U R Unique

and other stories

By Reva Rubenstein

Thank you Rabbi and Mrs. Lipschutz for granting me the
zechus to write for the Yated Ne'eman, and for your gracious
permission to reprint my stories here.

Cover design by Goldstar Graphics

ISBN 978-1-59826-001-4

FELDHEIM PUBLISHERS
POB 43163 / JERUSALEM, ISRAEL
208 AIRPORT EXECUTIVE PARK
NANUET, NY 10954
WWW.FELDHEIM.COM
PRINTED IN ISRAEL

For my family…

To Mom who says: There's a lesson in everything.

And to Dad – I write for you.

To my twin sister, Yehudis, for your good natured, intelligent, and accurate editing and proofreading, and for the overnight service.

And to my brother, Morris, my "publisher."

To Bubby and Zaidy: *mazal tov* on your sixty-fifth wedding anniversary -- until 120!

And thank you YSFMH, YL, SN, EC, DB, NN, LH and Dovid -- for your constant inspiration.

with endless love.
RR

Contents

Avital the Actress

"IT'S OFFICIALLY PLAY SEASON in Emunah Academy!" Avital said to Chava as soon as she opened her eyes Monday morning. "I am so excited! Aren't you?"

Chava, still half asleep, nodded her agreement. The sisters got dressed and went downstairs to eat breakfast. "I'm sure looking forward to finally being part of the senior class in the high school play," Chava said as she poured a bowl of cereal. "Twelfth graders are in charge of the choirs, dances and drama. And the best part is that we get to wear long, black gowns with sequins on the sleeves and multicolored sashes for the grand finale. It really is exciting."

"Chava," Avital asked nervously, "what do you think the chances are of my getting a part in drama? I'm just a ninth grader. Do you think they ever choose younger girls?" She took a bowl of cereal and looked anxiously at her older sister.

"Don't worry, Avital. I know you're a great actress, but don't set yourself up for disappointment. Everyone does something. You might be in a choir, or song-dance, or on the lighting committee or write the playbill. No one feels left out." Chava said kindly.

"Well," said Avital with a melodramatic sigh, "if worst comes to worst, I guess I'll have to just enjoy spending extra time with my friends during practice. But I would *love* to use my acting abilities." Avital's eyes grew dreamy for a moment. "I would love to stand in the middle of the stage and have the audience roar with laughter or cry with sadness because of something I said. What power! To carry other people's emotions in the fist of your hand – to be able to make them feel what you want them to feel, to struggle with you, to live with you! Remember last year, when you were the queen who was in captivity in the dungeon and at the last minute you managed to escape by climbing over the edge of the stage and running through the center aisle. The whole audience stood up to cheer. How did it feel?"

"I guess it felt good not to trip on that long satin gown when I was running. I just did what the director told me to do. Plus, when the drums are beating and the lights are low, that adds to the effect. And maybe after sitting for three hours the people were just happy to get up and stretch. You're so psychological, Avital."

"I know. I think if I'd get a part, I'd eat, sleep and become that character. I would live her life, dream her dreams, think her thoughts, until her every word felt like it was coming from my heart," Avital said.

"That would make it kind of hard to get through a regular day of classes and homework if you're a queen… or a soldier, or a tomato."

"A tomato?"

"You don't remember the year that Emunah Academy put on a nature play and between the scenes girls sang vegetable songs?"

"I don't think I could bear it," said Avital, placing her hand on her heart.

"Hey – it's only a play," said Chava.

But to Avital, it was much more than that.

Today was the day for try-outs. As the girls rushed to grab a hot mug of cocoa to take on the bus and hurried out the door, Avital paused to kiss the *mezuzah*. "*Hashem – please* help me get a good part! I really want to act!" And then she ran to catch the bus.

Three days later, the entire school gathered together to hear the schedule for practices and to find out who received which part in the play. "Please listen carefully," said Mrs. Grinvalt, the director, who the school imported each year from the city to direct the girls. "First, I will outline the plot of the play. Then you will divide into groups and start to practice with the twelfth graders assigned as your 'heads.'

"As some of you already know, we'll be putting a brand new play called 'The Last Winter' by R. Rubenstein." She glanced down at the script in her hand. "The setting is a small *shtetl* in White Russia in the midst of a cold winter during times of the Cossacks. The main characters are Yehuda and Sarah Reichenblit, and their children Mordechai and Gluckle, who are refugees from another town which was destroyed. The first scene finds them on an *erev Shabbos*, desperately searching for shelter on the edge of the town. Let me interrupt myself and say the props girls will enjoy setting up old shacks for scenery on that one."

She returned to the script. "The Reichenblits are quickly taken in by an old couple who have a mysterious past. They welcome the family into their shabby home. But we become suspicious during the second act when it's Shabbos and the unknown couple is so unfamiliar with *kiddush* and other *mitzvos*.

"The next day, Yehuda takes Mordechai to *shul*. This is a lovely scene. The first choir will sing *lecho dodi* with authentic Chassidishe tunes that have been preserved until today, and we may even throw in a dance. I think your school has a supply of *shtreimels* in the costume closet.

"Meanwhile, Sarah collapses at home due to the pressures she's been undergoing. When Yehuda and Mordechai return from their uplifting trip to *shul*, Sarah is sick in bed and Gluckle has disapppeared.

"At this point, we'll have a short scene in front of the curtain where we see Gluckle being kidnapped and taken to the local church. I think we'll get a snow machine to remind people that it's winter. It spews out scraps of paper or styrofoam, not real snow. I'll have to ask permission from the auditorium owners." Mrs. Grinvalt jotted a quick note on her paper and then continued the narration.

"A confrontation follows. Upon being accused of the kidnapping, the mysterious couple – who indeed are agents of the church – throw the Reichenblits out onto the streets. They are taken in by the Rabbi of the town who warns them they are in great danger.

"The search scene follows. While the Reichenblits are searching for their daughter, the long arm of the church is out to silence the Reichenblits. That will be the second dance. I think the search will spill off the stage and take place in the midst of the audience, but I don't think the fire code in the auditorium will allow us to give you candles for the search. We'll have to think of something else…

"In any case, after the search is the counter-kidnapping accomplished by the Rabbi's son. However, as he is returning Gluckle to her parents, a Cossack, named Anthony, is hot on Sarah's trail. Just as the Rabbi's son informs Yehuda and Sarah that he wishes to marry Gluckle, Sarah is killed by the Cossack's sword, while the rest of the family flees.

"A choir follows, and the words of their song explain that the couple, with Yehuda and Mordechai, escape to another *shtetl* and begin life anew. The final scene will show the birth of Gluckle's daughter, named for her mother. I just haven't decided whether we'll use a real baby or a doll for that last scene. Any questions, girls?"

"Uh, Mrs. Grinvalt," said Fraidy, a tenth grader with thick glasses sitting in the front row. "I think I recollect reading this same plot once, only the setting was in England in the 1800's. And instead of a girl being kidnapped, it was a whole school that was taken over by the church."

"And doesn't it remind you of the play we did in 9th grade?" said Chava. "That was a holocaust story, but the kidnapping and everything sound so familiar."

Estie interrupted her. "Only then, the father was the one that died, and the children escaped to Palestine which was just being established."

"I remember a few years ago when my older sister was in the play," Malka piped up, "and she was a Jewish girl in Spain. She was kidnapped as a baby and returned to her family only after the mother died looking for her on a farm. I still remember the real chickens they had on the stage for that scene."

A babble of voices erupted. Mrs. Grinvalt raised her hand for silence. "Girls. Let me step out of my role as play director for just a moment and pretend to be a history teacher. I will tell you that since Emunah Academy chooses to perform plays that are Jewish historical fiction --- *what do you expect?* This is Jewish history! We say it in the *hagada* every year: '*Bechol dor vodor omdim oleinu lechalosaynu!* In every generation, there are those who rise up against us and seek to destroy us, but *Hakodosh Baruch Hu* rescues us from their hands.' All the play-write has to do is change the setting and the enemy, and a few details – and you have a play.

"However, by acting, singing, and even attending the performance, the message that the school is teaching you in class is reinforced. *Hashem* protects the Jewish people in every time and every era. By choosing plays like *The Last Winter*, I think your school wants you to take that message to heart. If you ask me, it's a whole lot more meaningful than a bunch of singing vegetables. In any case, let me read the names of the girls who are in the cast, and then we're off to work."

Mrs. Grinvalt looked down again at her sheaf of papers and began to read, amidst much squealing and squawking, the names of the girls who were assigned to each part. "And, last but not least, as the main part: the lead character of Sarah Reichenblit will be played by Avital Sorovsky!"

As the girls got up to go to their assigned groups, Avital's eyes filled with tears. "Oh, thank you, *Hashem*!" she whispered, "and hello Sarah. Welcome to my life."

★★★

Play practice began to take over the lives of every girl in town, but none more than Avital Sorovsky. Each girl had to scramble to finish her homework early in order to be able to return to school at night for practice. Younger sisters suddenly found themselves standing in as babysitters, dishwashers, and general housekeepers while their older high school sisters were nowhere on the horizon. The family cars were often deployed in the call of duty, their newly minted drivers picking up wood to build shacks, or rolls of rough burlap for costumes, or branches to paint white so they would look snow-covered.

A committee of girls scoured the neighborhood, asking store owners for donations for their school in return for an ad in the playbill. Other girls spent hour after hour, bent over the school computers, typing up a list of the cast so that it could be printed along-side the ads. A lucky few students were driven after school each day to the local public school where the maintenance men showed them how to operate the lighting from a room that overlooked the auditorium. They received permission from the authorities to use the snow machine, a resounding 'no!' for the candle idea, and a warning not to allow snacks in the hall.

Everyone was busy. Teachers and tests, socializing and siblings, all had to stand aside to make way for the grand performance. The school was coalescing into a gigantic, unified dance and song troupe; each and every member of the student body gave as much time as she could to make 'The Last Winter' a memorable success.

But Avital gave more than her time. She gave her soul. Suddenly, everything about the Cossacks was of interest to her. In what little spare time she could muster, she researched the path that the looting, murderous Cossacks took across Europe, studying maps, trying to figure out where the Reichenblits may have lived and which direction they would have traveled toward safety. She studied which *gedolim* were alive during that era, and wondered who the Reichenblits may have asked for guidance. She read stories of heroism of men, women and children who gave up their lives just because they were Jews.

***

"Why are you making so much noise?" Chava suddenly asked Avital. "I've been trying to fall asleep for a half an hour and you keep on tossing and turning."

"I can't sleep," Avital said.

"Well, why not?" asked Chava. "Aren't you tired enough? Three hours standing on stage, repeating over and over, 'My child! Where is my precious Gluckle?' didn't make you tired enough to sleep?"

Avital turned her head toward her sister and sniffled.

"Avital?" Chava asked, suddenly concerned. "Are you okay? Did someone hurt your feelings? Or is the pressure of being the lead actress too much?"

"It's… it's not that. I'm just thinking of how scary it must have been for Sarah. First, to be chased by the Cossacks from her home, and then to lose her precious daughter. How did she survive?" Avital's eyes were filled with tears.

Chava sat up in bed and turned on the light. "Avital. The play is historical *fiction*. That means it never really happened, okay? There is no such person as Sarah Reichenblit. Give me a break. Just go to sleep, or I'll start worrying that something is seriously wrong with you."

"Okay, Chava. I know. I was just thinking. Good night."

Chava turned off the light, and soon both girls were breathing rhythmically. Only under her blankets, Avital was shaking. How would Sarah have slept, with the Cossacks so close, practically breathing down her neck….?

Evening after evening the girls dutifully made their way back to school for play practice. Groups of girls came by carpool and foot, laughing and chatting. Some complained that they had no time for homework, and not nearly enough time for shopping. Some discussed the dance steps, and some were singing snippets of the songs they were to going to perform. The school play dwarfed any other activities in the girls' lives.

Only Avital walked alone, clinging to the wall in the long hallway on the way to the auditorium. Every once in a while she would stop and glance around her, as if she were afraid.

"Hey, Avital," called Chava. "Wait up!"

Avital gave a startled jump, and then waited for her older sister.

"Mommy asked me to give you this snack since you have practice until really late tonight."

Avital stretched out her hand and grabbed the snack bag. "You have revived me," she croaked. She tore open the bag, said a fervent *bracha*, and devoured the chips.

"Uh, Avital. Maybe Mommy should have sent a whole dinner. You're really hungry, aren't you?"

"I've had no food all day. And yesterday, I had only a bowl of cold kasha," Avital said.

"What!? I saw you eat breakfast, lunch, and dinner! Dinner was just an hour ago! I watched you eat a piece of chicken, two servings of salad, and hey... you even ate a slice of cake for dessert!"

"In Russia," Avital said slowly, "we have no dessert." Then she turned, and continued her slow, careful, suspicious walk into the auditorium, just in time for scene three.

★★★

Avital stood in the hallway of her house on Friday afternoon and stared at herself in the mirror. She practiced the different emotions she would have to play. She lifted her chin up and down, throwing her shoulders forward and back, leaning her head on her arm, and then standing ram-rod straight, until she could masterfully play both a woman sick in bed, and a brave woman, setting out to search for her missing daughter.

"Avital? What in the world is the matter with you?" her mother asked as she rushed in with a bag of groceries. "You look awful!"

"Oh, I'm alright, Ma. It's just that they've robbed me of my home and now they've stolen my ..."

"Is this about the play?"

"Uh, sure, Ma. I was just saying that..."

"Avital, could you bring in a few more bags of groceries from the car, please. The play can wait, but Shabbos can't."

Avital went off obediently, but as she passed, her mother could hear her daughter whispering to herself, "I shall never give up. Though it may cost me my life..."

***

"Tatty," Avital asked her father at the Shabbos table that week, "does our family have any roots back in Russia? How about a great-grandfather from somewhere close by -- like Poland or Romania?"

Her father looked at her, puzzled. "Avital, you know that we're German Jews. Both my parents and your mother's parents are from Germany, and we go back more generations than we can count. I brought a *wimple* to *shul* when I was three years old, and we say all the *yotzros* in the back of the *Siddur*. Why in the world are you asking?"

"I just sometimes feel so close to the Jews who are descendants of Chassidim. You know, their songs are so beautiful, and their heritage is so rich, I feel like I could have come from there."

Her father looked even more confused. "You don't like our songs?" he asked.

"It's the high school play, Tatty," Chava explained. "I wouldn't even bother trying to bring our actress back down to earth. I'm just waiting for it to be over."

"Next week is the performance," Mommy added.

"I see," he said, rather doubtfully, and, casting a glance at his dreamy daughter, he went back to eating his bowl of *gruenkern* in peace.

***

Amidst all her bustling back and forth just before the performance, Mrs. Grinvalt made a special point to come over to Avital to compliment her on her acting. "In all my years directing plays, I have never seen a girl so enwrapped in her part. You have been an exceptional actress to work with, and I look forward to working with you in the future."

Avital smiled back, but she couldn't reply. If she'd agree with Mrs. Grinvalt that there would be other plays in the future, then Sarah would disappear in a ghost-like wisp. It was many hours too soon! First – the play!

The audience was hidden in the darkness. On cue, Avital walked onto the stage for act one, dressed in a brown dress, a knitted brown shawl draped around her shoulders, a flowered kerchief covering her hair, and wandered through the rubble that the props girls had scattered around the stage. Her back was bent, and she shuffled slowly in her heavy, leather boots as she crossed to the center of the stage where Mrs. Grinvalt had directed her to begin.

All she needed, so desperately, was a place to stay tonight, to get out of the bitter cold. She looked up at the white branches. Oh, the snow was freezing! All her feather blankets and pillows that she had scrimped and saved for were gone now... torn by the Cossacks' cruel swords that hungrily searched for treasures she did not own. But at least she had her husband, Yehuda, and her two precious children. She looked at them, gathered together in the center of the stage, with love in her eyes as she began her lines. She was Sarah!

Scene followed scene, song followed song, and dance followed dance, until finally the cruel Cossack, Anthony, who had followed Avital to the edge of town for the reunion with her daughter, caught up with her and pushed a collapsible sword into her back. Yehuda, Mordechai, Gluckle and the Rabbi's son ran off, stage right. Anthony ran off, wildly laughing, stage left.

Avital fell onto the floor with a cry. "I have been stabbed." Then she leaned on one elbow and began her last speech. "But far better to die for a cause than live with none! I have not lived in vain. I have no regrets! For I have given my life to my nation – that they shall live. This knowledge is my greatest reward!" Heaving a sigh, she screamed *"Shma Yisroel!"* and collapsed on the wooden floor.

The curtain closed as the audience went wild. Applause and cheering filled the hall. Meanwhile, behind the curtain, the props girls quickly pushed the trees on wheels off the stage and the entire school filed onto stage for the grand finale song.

Avital picked up her head, took a deep breath, and prepared to stand and receive her praise--and the dozen roses she knew were waiting for her. First, however, she closed her eyes for a brief moment and bid farewell to Sarah Reichenblit who had been her constant companion and inspiration for weeks during play season, and who lay on the floor, dead.

But although Sarah's voice was silenced, she would never really disappear. Sarah Reichenblit would live on forever in the depths of Avital's soul.

A Winning Strategy

THE FAMILIAR SOUND OF ARGUING filtered down through the floorboards to the kitchen where Mrs. Kasperof had just served her husband a late dinner after his hard day at the law office. When the noise began, the parents exchanged a cheerless look.

"Certainly ruins my appetite," Tatty sighed, as he lay down his spoon and looked at his soup sadly.

"I'm sorry, dear. Shall I put on a music tape to drown them out?"

"No, no more noise," he grumbled. "The courtroom was so noisy today that I could barely think."

The sound of a large crash made Mommy catch her breath. "Do you think that was the dresser, dear?"

"Or the night table," he replied. "I believe it's your turn to tame the natives."

"Today's Tuesday, then, isn't it? Oh, all right. The rest of your dinner is on the counter. I should be back in time for dessert."

"Thank you – and good luck."

Mommy pushed back her chair and headed for the stairs. Long ago, they had adjusted to their son Ronny and his vicious fighting, and they tried their best to deal with his eruptions, while at the same time protecting their other sons Sruly, Benny and Mendy, from Ronny's argumentative side. She sighed as she grabbed the clean laundry to bring upstairs on the way. Argumentative *side*? she thought to herself. His whole essence is arguing. What a difficult child!

"What are you boys doing?" she called out as she reached the top of the stairs.

Sruly came hurtling down the hallway towards his mother. "Save me! Save me!" he cried. "Ronny's going to get me!"

Mommy balanced the clean laundry basket under one arm and placed the other arm protectively around her oldest son. "Where is he?"

Sruly pointed to the room the four boys shared. "In…in there. But I wouldn't open the door if I were you…"

Mommy marched forward. "Parents can't afford to be afraid of opening doors," she said as she pushed open the door to the room – and gasped in disbelief as a *negel vaser* bowl full of water came spilling down from the top bunk, soaking the contents of her laundry basket.

"Ronny!"

"Mommy?!" came the surprised, timid reply.

"Look what you did! Now *you're* going to mop up the floor and then put all these clothes back into the dryer, fold them up neatly and put them away. Why in the world would you throw water on the laundry? And why is the dresser tumbled over on its side?"

"I thought you were Sruly," said Ronny as if that answered the whole question. He climbed down from the bunk, looking somewhat remorseful.

"And what if I were?" asked Mommy. "Since when do we play with water in bedrooms? Since when do we knock over furniture?"

"If you were Sruly," replied Ronny, "you'd be drowning in the *Yam Suf*. My horses had just made it through the sea, and Sruly was supposed to drown. The dresser is supposed to be the wall of water, and…"

"I didn't want to be Pharoah," Sruly suddenly spoke up. "He made me."

"I just said that you'd make a better Pharoah since you're bigger," said Ronny.

"Pharoah was short. I didn't want to play at all. I was in the middle of reading a book and you grabbed it away," said Sruly.

"You weren't reading. You were just looking at the pages."

"And to think –"Mommy interrupted, with a groan, "I actually *davened* for children. Don't you do anything besides argue?"

"Sometimes we have fist-fights," Benny offered from under the bed.

Mommy put down the basket, and folded her arms. "No more. Let's get this place cleaned up."

Sruly and Benny were dismissed to go keep their father company downstairs for the remainder of dinner, and Mendy was safely plunked into his crib, while Ronny wiped up the floor, picked up the dresser and separated the dry and wet laundry under his mother's watchful eye. As he worked, he kept up a running commentary of defense. "After all, what can you expect from a fourth grader who learns about Pharoah and fighting and drowning and swords and war chariots all morning in Yeshiva? Doesn't Tatty always say that Torah is our life? So what's a little water on the floor when it comes to learning?"

"If this game were all about learning, it would be one thing," Mommy replied. "But what about last summer when you insisted that you were a soldier and that your poor little brother Benny was the prisoner. You blindfolded him and marched him into the garage to contemplate his fate until we discovered that he was missing for dinner."

"Oh, that? In the summer, we were learning about the Roman soldiers attacking the *Bais Hamikdosh*. I thought that it would be a good idea to teach him about sieges and…"

"And then in the fall," Mommy continued, unconvinced, "you decided to be a king and banish poor Mendy from your 'kingdom' – and his crib – leaving him to sleep in the hallway. Tatty practically tripped over him in the middle of the night."

"We were learning about… um… Yaakov's dream. I think I gave him a pillow to sleep on…" Ronny felt his defense beginning to crumble.

Mommy looked into Ronny's dark, green eyes. "Ronny Kasparof. You have an answer for everything. I think you just like to fight and bully your brothers around. You're just too argumentative. It's time to grow up."

Ron sighed to himself as he took the wet laundry down to the dryer. He peeked at the hallway mirror as he passed by. Grow up, his mother had said. Ha! There was nothing he'd like to do more. But it was easier said than done. Sruly was lucky. He was tall for his age and was already the head of the fifth grade basketball team. Benny was tall, too, for a second grader. Even Mendy showed every sign of becoming a tall Kasperof, outgrowing his stretchies length-wise long before his tummy reached the limits of the snaps.

Ronny looked at himself and shook his head. Ronny the Runt, he snarled at the freckled face. The one thing he hated more than being shorter than the shortest kid in fourth grade was losing every race, game or contest in school and camp. Without the brawn, he decided that his brains would have to make him a winner. He would outsmart, outfox, and outthink anyone that came across his path. Ronny pushed the thick red bangs off his forehead and straight up into the air, pulled his *payos* out from behind his ears and snarled wildly at his reflection. No one would push around Ronny Kasperof – not if he could help it.

The room got clean, and the laundry dried and put away, but the arguing and fighting only got worse and worse. Any statement, by anyone, would be countered by Ronny…

At home: "It's time for school," Mommy would call.

"There's still four minutes until the bus."

In school: "The answer to the math problem is 54."

"I got 55."

To the radio announcer: "Rain today," said the weatherman.

"Not a cloud in the sky," Ronny would reply, shaking his fist.

And, worse of all, to his brothers: "The music is too loud," "No, it's not."

"You said you'd save me the last candy," "No, I didn't."

"It's my turn on the computer," "No, it isn't."

"You're not even arguing, Ronny," said Sruly one day. "You're just contradicting."

"No, I'm not," said Ronny with a frown.

★★★

"I think Ronny needs his own room," said Mommy as she and her husband sat down to their late night dinner. "Listen to what's going on!"

The parents silently stared at the ceiling as the voices from upstairs echoed downward.

"You did not ask permission to take my basketball to school!"

"Sruly -- I don't have to ask your permission. You're a *koton*. Since you're younger than *bar mitzvah*, nothing really belongs to you anyhow." His voice had a mean, teasing tone.

"So where is it now, Ronny? Did you lose it?"

"Where do *you* think it is?" Tatty could just imagine Sruly, backed into a corner, desperate for his beloved basketball, and Ronny, sidling over to him, ready for a fight.

"Tell me where it is, Ronny," Sruly begged. "Did you *lose it?*... Mommy!"

"I'm glad it's Wednesday. Your night," said Mommy as she turned back to her plate and bit into her tuna fish sandwich.

"I'm going, I'm going," said Tatty standing and brushing off his lap. Suddenly, his eyes turned bright. "But I have an idea. I'm going to take Ronny out shopping."

"But dear -- your dinner..."

"Put it in the fridge, please. I'm going to bring this arguing to an end for once and for all," said Tatty as he marched up to the battlefield.

"A zebra doesn't change its stripes," Mommy sighed after him.

"This zebra may stay striped, but the lines are going to run the other direction," said Tatty as he took the stairs two at a time.

"Ronny. Grab your jacket. We're driving over to Toy Town."

"It was a genuine championship basketball," Sruly said, following them to the door. "Make him pay for it, Tatty. He lost it."

"Basketball? Oh, right. Yes, we'll get a basketball for you, but I have something else up my sleeve."

A surprised Ronny put on his coat and followed his father out to the car. He waited for the speech to start, the one about getting along with his brothers, being more agreeable and learning to give in, but instead his father chatted about the *parsha* and the weather. By the end of the journey, Ronny began to perk up. Maybe, at last, his father was taking his side. Maybe he was getting a new toy for… Hhmmm. He couldn't quite figure out why – his birthday was long past, and Chanuka was a memory -- but who was he to argue with his father? Oh no, not him.

When they arrived at the store, Mr. Kasperof quickly picked out a basketball and then took Ronny right over to the shelf with games. "*Nu?* Do you see a chess set?"

"There, Ta. On the top shelf."

"Ah… got it. Oh, it's a nice one. Wooden pieces and a king without a cross on his head. And it comes with a book about winning strategies and gambits. You like it?"

"Well, uh, sure."

"It's a present for you, Ronny. You have everything it takes to be a good chess player. See what it says here on the box?" His father lowered his voice and read with emotion, making the brown, white and red box sound like it contained the most mysterious and engaging treasure. "'Chess: the game of champions. A game of attack and counter-attack. A game of skill and cunning.' This is just right for you, Ronny. If you like to argue, and you like to win, chess is the way to go. Want to try it?"

"Do I have to pay for the basketball?"

His father shook his head no.

Ronny was so relieved, he agreed to his father's stipulation -- that he'd dedicate a half an hour a day to learning how to play chess. On the way home from Toy Town, he read the small print on the box, how chess teaches children forethought and planning, abstract thinking, and mental discipline. He didn't particularly like the part about its use in teaching children the ability to handle defeat and good sportsmanship, since he didn't plan on losing. And the part about chess training children to take responsibility for their actions, to defer gratification and to practice patience was hardly the point, if you asked him!

His motivation was from an entirely different source. He knew, when he walked in the door, with the box under his arm, that if he practiced, he would have something at which he'd be able to beat his brothers -- and all the boys in his class -- without having to grow another inch. Ronny and his father shared an elated feeling that night. It seemed that Ronny was about to turn a corner in his life.

Sure enough, Ronny took to the game like a fish in water. Right away he learned how to set up the board, with the white square in the lower right hand corner. When he placed each queen on her own color and Sruly disagreed, saying it didn't make sense, he simply showed him the rules: Black queen begins on black, white queen begins on white. Nothing to argue about.

He went to sleep reading about checkmates, stalemates and castling. He memorized the algebraic notation for the game, laughing when he noticed that N stood for knight since K is already for king. He even played solitary chess games in bed at night, with a flashlight under the blanket.

Ronny quickly absorbed the different moves of each pieces:

the rock-like strength of the rooks as they slid vertically and horizontally across the board, the smooth diagonal grace of the bishops, the unfettered bounce of the knights, the stately power of the queen, and the dignity of the king. But most of all, he respected the small, straight-shooting pawns.

He read about how good players developed their own style. Little by little, game after game, he found himself holding on to his pawns. Other people might use the smallest pieces as sacrifices to achieve greater gains. Not Ronny. He felt for the pawns. Sure, they were small, but they were powerful. Each pawn that marched across the board, carried the potential for greatness: eventual kingship. In a Ron Kasperof game, it was surprisingly common for him to still possess six, seven or all eight of his pawns, in their original or altered state, at the closing of the game.

Three months after he was introduced to chess, he brought home an excellent report card – including an *aleph* for cooperation, the very first time in his schooling history. As a reward, his father offered him tickets to a regional chess match.

Ronny accepted the invitation eagerly, and the day arrived. "Come on, Ronny. You don't want to miss the opening of the game," his father called, keys in hand.

"Coming!" Ronny called. On the way out of the door, he quickly peeked in the hall mirror, brushed down his thick red hair, and tucked his *payos* neatly behind his ears. Ron the Pawn, he grinned to himself, and ran off to join his father.

★★★

"It's awfully quiet upstairs," said Mommy, bringing a plate of squash soup to the table for her husband at the end of his workday.

"Chess is quiet," Tatty replied as he helped himself to a handful of croutons. "I think Ronny's taught even Mendy how to move the pieces across the board by now."

Mommy paused, and suddenly said, "I never did figure out how you came up with the brilliant idea of buying him a chess set."

"Do you think I was always the sweet, reasonable husband you see seated before you today?" he asked, raising his eyebrows. "I practically drove my parents insane with all my arguing until my father started me on chess. Chess talent runs in the family, you know. Later, they sent me to law school to use my prodigious oral talents. Lawyers never argue, dear."

"They don't?"

"Oh no, no, no. We negotiate," he said slowly and firmly.

"Ah. I see," said Mommy, and at last, they enjoyed their meal in peace.

In Style

THE SUN BEAT DOWN ON THE HOT, BROOKLYN PAVEMENT, and the heat radiated upward, right through the soles of Bina's shoes. The pleasant spring weather that had accompanied Shavous the week before had vanished, leaving in its place a heat wave that hinted at a scorching summer ahead. Bina wiped her forehead as she trudged toward home, lugging her Regents books in her briefcase, mentally preparing for a long night of studying.

"There's only one thing keeping me sane," she comforted herself aloud as she climbed up to her second floor apartment. It's a good thing it's almost Sunday."

She walked into the apartment, said hello to her mother in the kitchen, and went to her room. First, she flipped on the air-conditioner. Then, she changed from her uniform sweater and heavy pleated skirt into a summer outfit. "Phew! Summer clothing is as important in the heat as winter clothes are in the cold! Well, time for dinner, and then I'll hit the books. And after two chapters, I'll treat myself to a phone call to Rifky. We have to finish our plans for Sunday..." she said as she walked into the kitchen.

"Hi, Bina. Talking to yourself again?" her younger brother, Moishe, asked. He was already sitting by the table, helping himself to a cold cup of milkshake.

"Hey, I'm my own best audience," Bina replied, sliding into her seat. "Do you want to listen to my Sunday plans?"

Moishe quickly shook his head, and returned to slurping his milkshake.

"Help yourself, Bina," said Mommy as she brought the noodles and cheese to the table. "And I'd like to hear your Sunday plans."

"Yum. I love *milchig*s. Thanks," Bina said, helping herself to a huge, overflowing plate of noodles. "About our plans: I decided that after all this studying I deserve a break. I called Rifky – remember I met her at the Chanuka party by Devorah's house? She's in twelfth grade and it turns out she's going to Camp Cool Cream, too. She offered to take me to her favorite store, so we're planning on taking the bus to the mall to shop for summer clothes. Mosambiques has a really great sale, and we need so many things for camp, we figured we'd start there. I never went before so I'm really psyched," Bina bubbled.

"Oh oh. Wait a minute..." she interrupted herself. Then she dumped half of the noodles back into the bowl. "If we're shopping on Sunday, I'd better be careful. You know, with this year's styles, even two pounds makes a difference."

"Huh?" asked Moishe. "You're skipping dinner now so you can fit into some skirt on Sunday, and *then* you're going to eat and bust out of it?"

"Well, no. I guess I won't eat afterwards either. I'll just be a smaller size and..."

"And never eat again? Boy, am I glad I'm not a girl." Moishe took the serving bowl. "Here. I'll eat your portion."

"Moishe, you've had quite enough," said Mommy, sliding the bowl away from his hands. "Time to say a *bracha achrona* and then go play. You have two hours until pajama time."

Moishe jumped up, wiped his hands on his pants, mumbed, "*ve'al hakalkala*," and dashed out the door, while Bina rolled her eyes. "And I'm glad that I'm not a boy," she laughed.

Mommy smiled. "I enjoy you both. But tell me something, Bina. Do you really think shopping in Mosambiques for summer clothes with Rifky is such a great idea? They do have a bit of an African look, you know. It's not so easy to find *tznius-dik* clothes there in the winter, and you may well be wasting your time to *shlep* so far by bus looking for summer clothes. You wouldn't want to try Faige's Fashion on the Avenue? Or Tzirel's Tznius Tops? I could find the time to go with you locally, if you'd like, and then we wouldn't have to worry about returns..."

"Ma! Yuck!" Bina shook her head. "I'm, like, not into that kind of clothes, you know what I mean?"

"No..." Her mother slid into a chair and looked at her daughter, puzzled. "No, I don't know what you mean. Go ahead. Explain."

"Oh, Ma. Explain?" She rolled her eyes again. "Like, I'm in tenth grade now. Like, I don't want to look like I walked off the streets of Brooklyn."

"But you *are* from Brooklyn. I think you look very nice. You don't look like you live on the streets to me."

"Ma, that's not the point. See, Rifky, she has a bit more, well, flair than, well, you... I mean, you and me. So I kind of thought that – Hey, don't be offended, Ma. It's just that I'm going to Camp Cool Cream with Rifky and she was there last year, so she knows the way girls dress there and I've heard so much about Mosambiques. Aren't you just dying to see what's there?"

Her mother shook her head. "Dying? No, I'm sorry. I'm afraid I'm not," she said dryly.

"You've got to trust me, Ma," Rifky said, standing. "I'm in tenth grade! If I don't know what's *tznius-dik* by now, when will you ever trust me to shop alone?"

"But Rifky's family may have a different set of standards than we do. Every family follows their own Rav, their own *minhagim* and customs, the rules of their school, and community..."

"Ma! She's doing me a favor! It's the chance of a lifetime!

What's wrong with being friends with Rifky?!" Bina's eyes narrowed, and she fought to keep her voice low.

"Of course she's your friend! I'm not saying anything about being friends.Okay, Bina," Mommy sighed. "I trust you. You can go."

★★★

Sunday was another scorcher. The sun hung heavy in the sky and the air felt like thick pea soup. The girls met by the bus stop and waited with a typical mix of Brooklyn society, a panorama of nationalities and accents. Bina and Rifky were the only ones dressed in clothing that covered their elbows and knees. After practically a week of dieting, Bina found herself dreaming of a cold ice cream cone.

"Freezing cold," she said aloud.

"Really hot day," replied an older woman holding a sun umbrella, giving Bina an odd look.

"Sure is," nodded a tall black man.

"It's supposed to be hot all week," Rifky volunteered.

"Well, let's hope it cools down by Memorial Day," said the man.

"Yeah, cool – but no rain on the barbeque," laughed another.

The bus pulled up, and all the people climbed on. Bina and Rifky found seats together and the bus lurched away from the curb.

"I'm having fun already," said Rifky.

"You mean the air-conditioning on the bus?" asked Bina. "It's yum!"

"Well, yeah, that too. But I mean, standing by the bus stop."

"Waiting by the bus stop in the heat was fun?"

"Not the waiting. The conversation. I like getting out of our own neighborhood and talking to different kinds of people. I think it's really interesting."

"Uh, talking about the weather?"

"It's more than that. I like mingling. That's why I like Mosam-

30

biques. Their clothes are cool. They don't make you look like, well, a girl that anyone would point to and say "she's *frum*."

"But... but I am *frum*," said Bina hesitantly.

"Yeah, but do you need to stand out like that? You'll see what I mean. Come on. Here's the mall."

The girls exited the bus and joined the colorful mobs of shoppers. Here was a place where the parking lot was filled long before the doors opened at 9:30 AM. Here was a place where throngs of people wiled away entire Sundays, buying and eating and pursuing entertainment. Here was a place that used more electricity in a day than the entire country of Zimbabwe uses in a year.

"I love this mall," said Rifky, as she jostled in amidst the crowd.

"Oh," said Bina, feeling more than a little lost. Rifky flew confidently down one hallway, up an escalator, and down another long hall, past a waterfall, and underneath an arch of streamers with Bina following breathlessly on her heels.

Finally Rifky screeched to a halt. "And here's Mosambiques!" she announced, throwing out her arms before a huge glass store front.

Bina stared at the shiny, metallic letters. They seemed to shimmer with a sort of holographic glow. "Wow!"

"It sure is 'wow,'" laughed Rifky. "Now look. I know this store like the back of my hand. How about if I shop around and pick up stuff to try on while you just kind of get familiar with the layout of the place. Meet me by the changing rooms over there, okay?" Rifky pointed to the left side of the store where there was a display of glittering coins strug across a doorway that was labeled "CHANGE."

"Oh, is that corny," groaned Bina.

"Come on, it's cute. Enjoy," said Rifky, and she disappeared behind a display of African bushmen.

Mosamabiques was bopping. The store was full of shoppers. The music had a definite African beat, and décor was a mixture of jungle and city, with vines hanging from street posts and oversized photographs of elephants and giraffes interspersed with subway stations. This certainly was not Faige's Fashion.

What was wrong with looking *frum*? Bina kept wondering as she touched the different fabrics and examined the price tags. "I never thought three was anything wrong with looking *frum*," she said out loud. "But maybe Rifky's right. Maybe I do look too *frum*."

"Pardon me, Ma'am?" said a sales woman, wrapped in what looked like a huge blanket, her hair piled on top of her head and twisted with straw. "You said you always look from... From what? The smaller sized to the larger? Or the larger to the smaller?" She stared at Bina, examining her from head to toe. "I think you'd fit right into our Troubled Teens' styles. Check out the rack on the left wall in the back," she said, pointing over her shouler.

Bina walked toward to T(2) sign hanging at a precarious angle on the back wall to 'check it out,' trying to look casual, as if she were perfectly at home in a store where the lights flashed on and off like the blinkers on her school bus. She examined the raggedy blue jean outfits. "Wow. I never knew people bought them pre-torn," she said aloud.

"You don't shop here often, do you?" said a teen-age punk next to her, treating her to a withering stare.

Bina shook her head. It was no use. She went to find Rifky by the changing rooms.

"How're you doing, Rifky?" asked Bina through the curtain.

"I've got a bunch of stuff to try on here. How 'bout you?"

"I think I need a little air. I'm going out to the hall for a few minutes. I'll be back. But don't leave without me," she added, suddenly worried.

"This pile is going to take some time," said Rifky's muffled voice. "See you soon."

Bina made her way around the racks and stepped out into the lobby. She found a small metal bench near the waterfall and sat down to rest, watching the water tumbling in an endless loop up and around and down. She found herself wondering if there was something the matter with her. Why couldn't she find anything in Mosambiques that she had even the vague desire to try on?

Suddenly, she saw a group of men, dressed in long white shirts and long white pants congregating around the waterfall. Behind them stood a number of women, wearing foreign looking clothing, and veils over most of their faces. A number of children were scattered about. The group arranged themselves all facing one direction, took off their shoes, and then suddenly they began to raise their hands and chant.

"Hey! Are they Arabs?" said Bina out loud. "Somebody – do something!"

"Shhhh..." said a man walking past. "They praying."

"Have some respect," said another passerby.

Bina shrank into her seat and watched the group all bow, then stand, and then suddenly kneel and bump their heads on the floor in front of them. The movements were repeated a few times.

Bina felt like she landed in a foreign country. She had never seen Moslem prayer before – and in public! When she was late to *daven mincha*, she would stand in a phone booth and pretend to be talking on the phone, rather than to have people think she was talking to herself. She gulped and looked around to see everyone else's reactions, but surprising, the mall-goers seemed to take it in stride. Some people stopped to watch, but most just rushed by to complete their chores.

After a few minutes, the people stood, said some more words, put their shoes back on, and dispersed. Bina got up and went to look for Rifky. She found her by the counter, waiting to pay.

"What'd you find?" Bina asked.

"Look – isn't this a go-o-orgeious shawl?"

"Well, it's kind of bright turquoise, isn't it?"

"I love it. And here's a skirt with an Indian pattern, and a top to match."

"You think all the beads will stay on in the wash?"

"Hmmm... I didn't think of that. Well, maybe I'll leave it then. But look at this," she said, holding up a jacket with fringes on the bottom and peace symbols on the arms.

"Interesting," said Bina with a cough.

"And this skirt is so soft..."

"Looks a little short, Rifky," said Bina. Suddenly, she had enough. What was wrong with looking like *frum* girls? If the Moslems could wear their special clothing – and pray in public too – wasn't she allowed to be proud of who she was? Couldn't she stand up for what she had been taught for years, that a girl's clothing should be refined and dignified, honoring her important position in the Jewish nation? Why should she try to fit in to clothes that were "the latest"? Why in the world would she even want to?!

"See, I want people to respect me as an individual," Rifky was saying.

"So you want to dress the way everyone else in this mall dresses?"

"Well, I don't want a taxi driver to pick me up and say, 'Where do you want to go? Brooklyn?' You know what I mean?"

"You might get home that way," said Bina thoughtfully.

"That's not the point. Look, I'm sorry if you didn't find anything here. You want to try another store in the mall?"

"It's been a lot of fun, but my feet are aching, Rifky. I'll help carry your bags and we can catch the bus home. And you know what I'd love to do?" she said, as they made their way down the elevator and out to the steaming street.

"What?" asked Rifky as they climbed the steps to the bus.

"Let's go out for ice-cream!"

"To celebrate my successful trip!" said Rifky, plunking down in a seat and hugging her packages.

"Yes," thought Bina, "a very successful trip." And for once, she didn't talk out loud. She had learned to listen to her own inner voice.

GPS

H E LOOKED AT HIS HANDS, WAITING -- waiting for quiet from the 11th grade class, in room 318, which swirled around him in perpetual motion. He would wait. He knew that eventually they would quiet down. One of the more conscientious boys – probably Zelig – would feel the teacher's disapproval and shout at his classmates – "*Nu!* Mr. Lynch is waiting already!" – and slowly the roar would subside. He would wait until then, before launching into the intricacies of force, mass, and acceleration. The laws of physics wouldn't change while he waited.

He looked at his hands. They were more wrinkled than he remembered. Paths of lines crisscrossed around the fingers. The knuckles bulged more, with wrinkles furrowing deep into the knobs. The fingers weren't opening as wide as they used to, he thought. Muscles didn't pull as hard, and the fingers were content to curl slightly inward, without stretching to their full length. And was there a slight tremor? He firmly placed his hands down on the desk and looked around the classroom. Zelig was reining in the troops. In a minute Mr. Lynch would begin.

A sigh passed his lips. How many more years would he teach physics, he wondered. He had been teaching in Yeshiva Toras

Noam for forty-two years already. Goodness – he was already a fixture in the school. He had seen two principals come and go, and had been working under Rabbi Berg for over a decade by now.

Things had changed. The boys were taller – or was he shrinking? There was a soda machine in the hallway and a closed-circuit security video camera by the main front doors. The physics lab was also new, with computers set up along the perimeter. The lab was only a part of the whole east wing of the building which had been added on. He had attended the dedication of the east wing with Mrs. Lynch. How delighted she had been with the success of the Yeshiva.

Of course, he remembered the original ground breaking ceremony of the old, brick building too: Rabbi Shanken, and Rabbi Weiss sitting up on the make-shift dais, and Rabbi Silber shoveling the first clod of earth. He remembered the clods of earth at Mrs. Lynch's funeral also…

"Uh…Mr. Lynch? Are you okay?"

It was Zelig who jolted him out of his reverie. "Thank you, boys. I appreciate a quiet audience."

Snickers from the back left corner. Without looking, Mr. Lynch knew it was Chaim. There was a Chaim in almost every class: the boy who would take advantage of a teacher's weaknesses. After so many years, Mr. Lynch accepted Chaim's type as part of the job description of teacher, and wasn't fazed by any of his disturbances.

Mr. Lynch adjusted his *yarmulka* on his nearly bald head and tapped the marker on the board. "Count down to the Regents exam: Four months and three weeks. Shall we begin?" He opened the marker, which worked almost as well as the old white chalk on the extinct blackboard, and began to write the day's formula.

★★★

One Tuesday afternoon in February, the class was half empty. "Where is everyone?" asked Mr. Lynch, disappointed. He had so much wanted to explain the third law of motion, and didn't want to have to repeat himself the next session.

Zelig spoke up. "Uh…it's snowing out, Mr. Lynch."

"Yes. And so…?"

"Well, a lot of kids live far away, like an hour from Yeshiva, and their parents said they should head home early if it looked like a blizzard might come."

Mr. Lynch shuffled slowly to the window. A blizzard? Sure enough, the snow was piling up fast and the sky was as white as the board. "What did Rabbi Berg say?" he asked.

Chaim answered loudly. "He said anyone who didn't have transportation home could leave early, so a bunch of parents came to pick up their sons. Me, I have my parents' car here, so I can't go until the end of this period."

Avrumi turned to Chaim. "You have your parents' car!? Can I have a ride?"

Mr. Lynch coughed. "Boys?" but he was hardly heard above the voices of the other twelve students who still remained in class.

"Can I have a ride?" Ephraim asked.

"Me too," added Nosson.

"Please… I didn't bring boots," Duvie begged.

"Well, I didn't bring a coat," pleaded Meyer.

Mr. Lynch coughed again and tapped the marker. "Boys, I will end class ten minutes early so you can discuss travel plans. Now, we have material to cover. Two months until the Regent exams. Frankly," he added quietly, with a worried look toward the window, "the weather looks somewhat unsafe."

He opened the text book and began.

Sure enough, a full twenty minutes before the bell was scheduled to ring, Mr. Lynch announced the end of the lesson. The class circled around Chaim like vultures, each looking for a possible opening to advance his case, to be one of the lucky passengers.

"I *did* help you with the last physics exam," said Ephraim.

"I'll help you with the next exam," begged Nosson.

"I'll buy you a can of coke every day for the rest of the week," offered Duvie.

"There's not going to be school for the rest of the week," sneered Meyer.

"My parents know your parents since before we were born," whispered Sruly in a desperate attempt to avoid a snowy walk home.

The clamoring around Chaim grew louder and louder. Finally, Chaim, who was clearly enjoying being the center of attention, raised his hand for silence. "Listen guys." Instant silence. "My parents' van can only hold seven, and they made me promise that everyone would wear seatbelts if I'd drive in the snow. I count as one, so it's only fair that the six boys who live the farthest from school can come with me. That's Zelig, Nosson, Moishy, Chezkail, Yitzy and Gavriel. Sorry, everybody else. Maybe another time."

Mr. Lynch watched as the remaining boys turned disappointedly and began to bundle up. Outside the snow was swirling around. One by one, the unfortunate boys left the classroom. In a few moments, they came into view from the third floor classroom window. Mr. Lynch leaned on the window sill and watched as each boy was swallowed by white and was lost from view.

Chaim stood with the lucky six by his desk. "So what's the order? Who gets driven first?" asked Moishy.

"Yeah. Which way are you going to go?" echoed Gavriel. "Over the bridge or under the highway?"

"Never fear," announced Chaim, and from his briefcase, he pulled a leather bag with a zipper. "My parents let me take the GPS. We'll just input all the addresses, and it'll chart the route for us."

The boys crowded around. Even Mr. Lynch came slowly closer. Funny. When he was younger, he remembered spending lots of time figuring out which route to take to where. After a family *simcha*, the relatives would endlessly discuss which bridge was the fastest to leave the city, or which highway would get them home first. It was almost part of saying good-bye, that figuring... sharing expertise of the roads and their conditions. He could almost hear Uncle Zalmy telling Uncle Ben about the shortcut through the city streets, and Aunt Bessie rolling her eyes and countering it with ask-the-policeman-for-directions stories.

Chaim's voice broke into his reverie. "I've got all your addresses in here. Now I hit "plan route," and there it is: analyzing 342598 roads, and presto! It comes up with the fastest way to get everyone home. Come on, guys. Let's go."

The boys left in a cluster. Mr. Lynch watched from the window. It took a moment until they rounded the building and appeared below. Snow swirled around them as they jostled each other and ran toward the parking lot.

Suddenly, they all stopped. Zelig was motioning toward the building. There seemed to be a discussion, a bit of shoving, a boy wildly gesturing, another one shouting, a boy pushed into the snow, and then slowly backing off into the midst of the blizzard, and then Zelig ran back. He must have forgotten something. Mr. Lynch turned to scan the classroom. Had Zelig left something on his desk?

Seconds later, the boy burst through the door. His cheeks were bright pink, and he was breathing hard.

"Uh...Mr. Lynch. How are you getting home? It's really tough out there, and Chaim's car is the last one in the parking lot. The boys sent me back to ask if you'd like a ride."

Mr. Lynch tilted his head to one side in thought. "Why, thank you, Zelig. But there aren't enough seat belts for another passenger."

"Uh... um...Moishy decided he wanted to walk," replied Zelig, looking at the ceiling.

"Well, if Moishy's walking, then I will take you up on your kind offer." Mr. Lynch pulled on his galoshes, bundled up in his overcoat, wrapped his scarf carefully around his neck, took his hat from the hook and placed it squarely over his *yarmulka*, took his umbrella in one hand, and his attaché case in the other, and followed Zelig out the door.

If anyone had been watching from the window of classroom 318, he would have seen an old man, surrounded by a group of teen-age boys slowly being escorted to his ride home. One boy would be seen carrying a black, leather attaché case, and another would be chasing a black hat in the snow. And then, they too, would disappear into the storm.

★★★

Chaim looked at his hands, waiting... waiting until Mr. Lynch would finish buckling his seatbelt and they could get started. He watched his own hands grip the steering wheel, loosen, and then grip again. Of course it was the "right" thing to do, to add this elderly teacher to his passenger list for the way home. It just wasn't his idea of fun. All afternoon he had waited to be the captain of the ship, the lone member of the class with access to a car. He looked forward to the thrill of ferrying each student back to the safe shore of his home, and now the wind was fast being taken out of his sails. How often did his parents let him take the car to Yeshiva? It was only because he lived so far away and the weather report scared them into thinking that busses might not be running that they reluctantly gave in, so they wouldn't be forced to drive carpool. And here was Mr. Lynch putting a damper on the fun.

"Mr. Lynch, if you give me your address," Chaim said as politely as he could, "I'll add you to the GPS system."

Mr. Lynch obliged, and the machine went into recharting mode. In moments, it adjusted the original route, leaving out Moishe's stop and adding in Mr. Lynch's.

"Very interesting," muttered Mr. Lynch. "The satellites that were originally launched into space to be used by the military to find objects in the dark, locate downed pilots, spy and map enemy movements have become civilian tools. Of course," he said, thinking out loud, "you would need three coordinates to locate the navigator itself in time and space. The system would have to detect how far away I am from each point, and how fast I'm traveling in order to know where I'm headed. Let's see… to cover the entire world you would need about 25 satellites, circumventing the planet at roughly…"

"Mr. Lynch?" Chaim interrupted, "I think they're up to 31 satellites now… a few for back-ups. So," said Chaim with a lilt in his voice, "if you're all buckled up, I'm ready to go." He put the GPS in the front window in its suctioned holder, and they were off.

"Turn right," the mechanical voice instructed Chaim. Chaim turned the car to the right. As he turned, he noticed Mr. Lynch, sitting next to him, grab the dashboard.

"You took that turn a little fast, Chaim," said Mr. Lynch.

Chaim just sighed. Of course they couldn't have left Mr. Lynch alone in school. How *would* he have gotten home in the storm? Maybe he would have slept in the classroom? From the look of things, the whole town would be closed down tomorrow. The streets were already practically empty now at 3:30 in the afternoon. Snow piled up on his windshield faster than the wipers could clear it, and the world around the car was silently readying for a nap under its fresh blanket.

"In two hundred feet, turn left, and then stay in the right lane. You have reached your first destination."

"Wow!" said Gavriel. "That GPS is so cool. Well, Chaim. Now that you know where my house is, come visit some day. Thanks a lot. Bye, guys. See you…" Gavriel climbed out the door and slammed it behind him.

"Turn left and proceed to light. Then turn left."

"I think I'm the next stop," said Nosson. "From Gavriel's house, my father usually takes the highway one exit," he added.

"Well, the GPS says we should stay on local roads, so I'm going to listen to him," said Chaim.

"It's a smart thing to do in the storm," offered Mr. Lynch.

"You never know if the highways are cleared."

"Mmmhummm," grumbled Chaim.

"Hey. Let's trip up Mr. GPS," said Nosson suddenly. "Let's see what happens if we don't listen to what he says to do."

Chaim's natural grin returned to his face. "You got it. Let's see... here we go."

"*Turn right*," said the GPS. "*Proceed down the block...*"

Chaim continued to drive straight. True, it was snowing, and he had to get these kids home, but this was too good of an experiment to miss.

"*Turn right now and go around the block*," said the GPS, adjusting to Chaim's supposed error.

Chaim went straight again.

"*Turn right now and go down two blocks,*" said GPS. Was there a bit of an edge in its voice? Was it getting nervous?

Nosson laughed out loud. "That machine really thinks on its feet. Look how it just readjusts its directions automatically. I wonder if it's going to eventually call you a dumbbell or something."

Chezkail joined in the mirth. "I can just hear it: *Turn right, man! I said turn right! What's with you anyways? How did you pass the driver's test?*"

Chaim chuckled. "Can you imagine the people who programmed it? How many chances do you think old GPS will give me before he shuts down and decides I'm just teasing him?"

Mr. Lynch coughed. "Chaim? I think now's not the time to find out. Please proceed to Nosson's house with the shortest route possible." His voice sounded very school teacher-y. It was clear he had no interest in trying the patience of the GPS.

Chaim sighed.

"*Turn right*," said the GPS, with instructions from the third readjustment.

Chaim obeyed. Within a few minutes, Chaim slowed down to a stop. The car gave an extra jerk, and then came to rest in front of Nosson's house. "Well, here's your place, Nosson. Sorry so quick."

Nosson opened the door. "That's alright. I was getting hungry anyhow. Say! It's getting slippery out here. Take it easy, Chaim, and thanks a lot." Nosson was lost in the flurry of whiteness, and Chaim pulled away from the curb.

"Do your wipers go any faster?" Mr. Lynch asked Chaim.

"No."

"Visibility's not great, you know," Mr. Lynch said.

"Yeah, I know. So, we'll get you home soon, okay?" Chaim's teeth gritted. It was hard to drive in the thickening blizzard. The last thing he needed was a backseat driver sitting right next to him in the front seat. "Chezkail and Yitzy? Do you think I can drop you both off at one place so I can get Mr. Lynch here home a little faster?"

The boys looked at each other and shrugged. Certainly, they would have preferred house stops, but, as guests in Chaim's car, could they argue? "No problem," they said in unison.

"Proceed to the intersection and then stay in the right lane. Stay in the right lane." The GPS sounded so sure of himself. Chaim revved up the engine and drove along in the right lane. It was a good thing, this GPS, he thought. It *was* becoming harder to see, and he was in unfamiliar territory.

"Go right," "Go left," "Proceed through the intersection, and turn left."

Chaim reached Yitzy's house. "Can you walk from here, Chezkail? Or maybe Yitzy's mother can give you a ride home?"

"My mother never drives in the snow," said Yitzy. "After hitting a mail box two years ago, a telephone pole last year, and the Rosh Yeshiva's brand-new used van at the beginning of the winter, she hangs up the keys on a hook the moment the first white flake appears. But maybe you can sleep over, Chezkail?"

The two boys climbed out of the car and continued their discussion as they slid toward the house.

"Only two more stops," announced Chaim. "It's you, Mr.

Lynch, and then Zelig, who lives around the corner from me. You doing okay, Mr. Lynch?"

"I'm fine, Chaim. But you should slow down. You know that today's lesson was about how kinetic energy increases with the square of the velocity."

"Huh?" Chaim wrinkled his forehead. He certainly *didn't* know that. He had spent the lesson fiddling with the GPS system inside his desk.

"What we mean is that the faster a body of mass is traveling the more dangerous and damaging any collision will be. If the same body of mass is proceeding at, say 5 miles per hour, it will cause…"

"Mr. Lynch. I don't plan on crashing, okay?"

"Turn right," interrupted the GPS. Chaim took the turn, and his back wheels skidded to the left. He quickly turned the same direction as the skid and the car straightened out.

"Slow down, Chaim," said Mr. Lynch firmly. "Do you see what's happening, Zelig?" he asked, addressing the only other passenger in the car.

"Uh…it's getting slippery, right?" said Zelig obediently.

"What's happening is that the friction is being reduced since the snow is making the surface of the road smoother than normal. Chaim had better slow down."

Chaim set his chin firmly, and continued to drive. Suddenly, Mr. Lynch reached out and flipped Chaim's hat off his head and into the back seat.

"Hey! What was that for! That's not safe!" complained Chaim loudly and angrily.

"A body in motion continues in motion until acted on by another force," replied Mr. Lynch. "You weren't listening to me, so I had to act."

Chaim slowed down, but he was glowering. It was hard enough for him to listen to teachers during school. Physics was just one of those subjects he sat through out of obligation. Now if this teacher was going to boss him around in his own car…! "Mr. Lynch," said Chaim, with a huge amount of self-control and *derech eretz* ingrained in him from infanthood, "I will drive slower, but you have to promise not to keep giving me instructions. We're not in school, and I'm the driver, and I'm finding it kind of difficult to drive with a physics lecture running in my right ear. You're almost home, okay. Can we have a quiet drive from now on?"

Chaim couldn't believe that he had the guts to say it, but he really *did* want to get home safe, the storm really *was* getting worse, and Mr. Lynch really *was* driving him crazy.

He stole a glance at the elderly teacher. Mr. Lynch sat quietly. "Okay, Chaim. I'm sorry. It's a deal."

★★★

Mr. Lynch stared down at his gloved hands. He hadn't meant to be a nudge, but this boy didn't have the years of experience he had driving in the snow. He'd try hard to be quiet now, to let the boy drive on his own, and to mind his own business.

"Go straight and proceed to the next corner."

Mr. Lynch glanced out the window. "That's funny," he thought. "I would have taken this turn here…." But the GPS was in charge and Chaim was the driver.

"Turn and proceed forward…"

"Wait a minute! I think we're heading over the bridge," thought Mr. Lynch. "But I live on this side…"

"Go forward five hundred feet and then make a right," commanded the GPS.

"Chaim!" shouted Mr. Lynch. "Don't….!"

CRUNCH!

"…Go over the side of the bridge," ended Mr. Lynch with a groan.

"Wha—wha—what happened?" whispered Chaim.

"You hit the guard rail. Obviously the GPS malfunctioned due to atmospheric pressures. The satellite system isn't flawless. Nothing is… nobody is," ended Mr. Lynch.

"Good thing I wasn't good too fast," said Chaim with a very small scared voice.

Mr. Lynch, Chaim, and Zelig sat in the car for an hour, waiting for the tow truck to come and pull them back to town. They talked about physics and driving and baseball and Yeshiva Toras Noam's history and by the time the tow truck came, they were fast friends. They all proceeded to Chaim's house, to buffer his parent's reaction, and to remind them how much they had to be thankful for.

"It was only the front bumper," said Zelig.

"And we were all wearing our seatbelts," said Chaim.

"And he really wasn't going too fast," added Mr. Lynch.

"By the way, Mr. Lynch," asked Chaim, as they waited for the taxi to take him home, "how *were* you planning to get home anyways? What would you have done if Zelig hadn't run back for you?"

"Oh, that," smiled Mr. Lynch. "Rabbi Berg was parked around the corner. He gives me a ride home every day. I just thought you boys could use a chaperone."

Mr. Lynch stretched out his hand, and met Chaim's hand for a warm handshake. His hands shook, true. But they could still point the boys in the right direction.

Then he waved, wrapped his scarf around his neck, and shuffled slowly toward the taxi in the snow, his attaché case in one hand, and his umbrella-turned-cane in the other.

Owls vs. Larks, and a Kick of Caffeine

"WHY CAN'T THERE BE 68 HOURS A DAY?" complained Sarah.
"How about 113?" countered Gittel. "Anything would be better than the mere 24 hours that we've got!"

"That's the truth," Sarah agreed. Her dark eyes flashed, as she pushed her black hair into place and adjusted the strap on her backpack. "This thing weighs a ton! I have my *chumash*, my math book, my literature book, my English grammar book, and my loose-leaf in here... all for this week's finals!"

"Then next week is *navi, halacha, tefila*, biology, and U.S. history," groaned Gittel, as she packed book after book into her already bulging bag.

"And we top off the schedule with Hebrew language, and Jewish History the following week," wailed Sarah, slinging her weighted backpack over her shoulder. "Ow! I wonder if my back will hold up...let alone my brain!"

The girls left the classroom and headed out toward the buses. "I'll speak to you later, Sarah," called Gittel, as she boarded her own bus. "What time should I call?"

"No time's too late in my house. We're all night owls," said Sarah with a smile.

"Really?"

"Sure. See, my mother works as a night nurse in a hospital. Three nights a week, she's out of the house. The other nights, she's so used to staying up late, she lets us join her. We always say it's too bad school starts in the morning instead of at noon. Anyways, how's 10:00 tonight?"

"I…I guess so. Sounds a little late to start," Gittel worried.

Sarah just laughed. "In my house, 10:00 is the middle of the day!" she called out the window as the bus pulled away.

"Middle of the day," muttered Gittel as the bus pulled away in a cloud of smoke. "I hope I can keep my eyes open by then."

The late night *chumash* study session was not such a great success. Gittel began by reading a *pasuk* and translating, but Sarah asked her to repeat. "I can't hear you, Gittel," Sarah confessed. "My sisters are laughing too loudly in the background, and… oh, my brother just came in from night *seder*. Hi, Benzy! Yeah, the tortillia chips are in the cabinet. Mommy and Tatty went out to a *chasuna*. Go ahead, Gittel. Sorry… you want to read again?"

Gittel managed to plunge ahead a few *pesukim*, amidst various interruptions. Finally, she placed her *chumash* on the kitchen table, and asked Sarah to take a turn reading.

And that's where her mother found her in the morning: still dressed in yesterday's uniform, with her blond, curly head resting on the kitchen table, an open *chumash* patiently waiting by her head, and the phone, lying beside her --off the hook.

"Gittel'le! What happened?" her mother asked with concern.

"Uh… What time is it? Morning already? I guess I fell asleep in the middle of studying. And I wonder if I really learned anything." Gittel got up and washed *negel vasser* in the kitchen sink, and rubbed the sleep out of her eyes. "Well, I guess I'll find out soon enough. The *chumash* final is first thing this morning. We have to *daven* at home today."

Her mother's eyes followed her with concern as Gittel struggled to stand, and headed upstairs to change and get ready for school.

***

"How did it go?" asked Sarah. "Did you get that section with the matching? It was so easy, wasn't it? That was exactly the part we studied last night! I was so glad we didn't study for nothing!"

"Well, studying for *chumash* is never 'for nothing,'" Gittel said righteously, "but which part are you talking about? I didn't get *any* of those matching questions."

"Yeah, come to think of it, you were awfully quiet at the end of our conversation. Like, around midnight, I began to wonder if you were listening at all. Then Fraidy clicked into our phone call with a question, and when I came back, the line was silent. I was afraid to call back and wake your parents, so I finished studying on my own."

"What time did you finish?" asked Gittel curiously.

"Oh, I think I remember seeing the clock at 3:00 AM as I said *Shma*," Sarah replied.

"Sarah," said Gittel, turning to her friend, "if you went to sleep at three o'clock in the morning, how come you're so wide awake now? I'll admit I dozed off somewhere in the middle of our conversation last night, and even so, I'm zonked!"

"Well, I did start the day with a pretty strong cup of coffee," Sarah said. "Plus, I didn't *daven* yet. I guess I'd better get going on that." Sarah pulled a *siddur* out of her briefcase to begin. "How about same time tonight to study for the math final, Gittel?"

"Well... I guess so," Gittel answered. "Unless you think you'd be available just a little earlier?"

"Okay, 9:45 it is. But Gittel," Sarah suggested gently, "maybe you should try to get in a nap today. You look kind of washed out." As she turned enthusiastically to her *siddur*, Gittel obediently nodded her head in agreement.

That afternoon, after school, Gittel lay down on her bed to rest up for the night's session. She tossed one way, and then the other. "I'm just not used to sleeping when it's light out," she thought. Then she smiled to herself, as she thought of her father's nick-name for her: Little Lark. Since she was a tiny baby, she was always up at the crack of dawn, singing for breakfast.

She could still remember as a small child, waking up in her lemon-yellow bedroom, and watching the sun shine in through the small eyelet holes of the curtains, creating sparkling patterns just for her. Once in a while, when her father wasn't in a rush, he would take her little hand in his and together they would go for an early morning walk. Ah! The pure joy of an untarnished morning. She vividly remembered the spring mornings: birds chirping and twilling, squirrels scampering for their morning meal, the sun brightly illuminating dew drops on the spider's webs left over from busy nighttime spinning. And the winter mornings: the snow sparkling fresh from a night's storm, covering trees and streets, with only her own footprints, next to her father's, breaking the vast whiteness. The beauty of an early fall morning: the newly fallen leaves still fresh on the ground, before being crushed by the day's traffic, the sight of early flocks flying toward their winter destinations… And best of all, the unbeatable joy of an early summer morning -- the sun's bright glare visible long before its midday fury and late night's stifling heat. Morning is the only time to enjoy a summer day, thought Gittel. And the smells….

Suddenly, her smile faded. Good-bye beautiful mornings. It was finals season. The pressure was on, and she would have to stay up late at night to study. She couldn't burn the candle at both ends. Or could she?

★★★

That night, Gittel sat down with her math book and dialed Sarah at promptly 9:45. "Hi. You ready?"

"I have to call you back in a few minutes. My cousin just walked in with a cake, fresh out of the oven. Want to start the first example in the meantime?"

"Sure, okay. But don't forget, I'm sitting by the phone."

A very long half an hour later, Gittel dialed Sarah's house

again. "How was the cake? You ready yet?"

"Sure. Sorry... I had to listen to the latest CD my cousin brought with her. She's going now... Bye, *Shuli*!" Sarah interrupted herself. "Okay. Where are you up to? Example 6?"

The girls struggled together to make the little numbers on the page behave the way they were supposed to. Sometimes they added up just right, but too often they had an annoying habit of getting in each other's way, putting their square roots where their fractal trees should be, and finding their way to the back of the page in long, drawn out division, when all they were supposed to do is march up to the top and sit demurely, smiling, with no remainders, like good whole numbers do. "Gittel," said Sarah, "I think the answer at the back of the book is wrong on this example. We've done it three times, and come up with three different answers."

She waited for a reply. "Gittel? Gittel? Are you sick of math? Are you crying? What's the matter?"

"I... I think I'm just really tired, Sarah. It's already 1:00 in the morning. My whole family is fast asleep. You mind if I quit now?"

"Well...okay, I guess. Good night, then. I'm going to call Fraidy and see if she figured this one out, and I'll let you know tomorrow."

"Okay. Bye, Sarah." Gittel used her remaining strength to replace the phone in its holder, and stumble up to bed.

★★★

The math test was behind her. Gittel sighed with relief as she passed her papers forward to her teacher's waiting hand. Math was one of her favorite subjects, and she thought she did pretty well, even though she konked out in the middle of last night's studying.

But tomorrow was literature and English grammar combined. All those long stories, with endless descriptions, famous foreign writers and six syllable vocabulary words! It looked like tonight would be another late one.

"You want to come sleep over, Gittel?" asked Sarah. "I mean, it looks like we're going to be up pretty late."

"Okay. That sounds great," Gittel replied. "I'll see you after dinner."

"Just make sure you're having *milchigs*," Sarah said.

"Sounds like you have a great dessert hiding in the freezer!" guessed Gittel, licking her lips.

"Yes, we have ice-cream, but I have another treat I'd like you to try," said Sarah with a mysterious smile.

Gittel arrived at Sarah's house with a small overnight bag and her briefcase. This was a nice vacation, she thought, after such a hard week. Maybe after they finished studying literature they'd have a chance to just shmooze. Maybe she'd even wake Sarah up a little early, and share the feeling of tomorrow's precious morning with her friend.

Why had she bothered to hope? In Sarah's house, it was impossible to get to work earlier than 10:00. First her little siblings had to be frolicked with, cared for, fed, bathed, and fed again… and, at long last, plunked into crib and bed. Then the older kids came home from their various activities, and married siblings checked in for the latest news and nibbles. At 10:00, Sarah and Gittel managed to find a space on the dining room table to set up their books and begin.

They turned page after page, testing each other on words like "stimulation" and "irritable" and "fatigue" from a story about astronauts. Finally, they discussed the character development. "So, we find in this story that the hero actual serves a dual purpose," Sarah read from her notes. "From his green eyes, you can tell that he misses the green earth even though he's far away, and…"

"Sarah," Gittel interrupted. "How can you prove that the author meant any of that? I mean, maybe he just gave the character green eyes because he likes the color green. I'm getting a headache from all this stuff."

"I think you're ready for a treat," Sarah said, sitting back in her chair, sizing up her friend. "Come on."

Together they went into the kitchen. Gittel looked longingly at the freezer. She *was milchig* after all, and ice-cream was one of her favorite foods. However, Sarah went straight to the stove and filled a tea kettle with water.

In minutes, the water boiled. Sarah opened a cabinet and took out a jar with a red label. She unscrewed the lid, and took a deep smell. "Aaaah! Here, smell this, Gittel."

"Hmmm. Coffee?" she asked.

"Yep. This is the best brand."

"I don't really drink coffee, you know," said Gittel. "I never have a problem waking up in the morning."

"Oh, my poor friend. You are missing out on one of the finest things in life." With an all knowing air, Sarah launched on a sales speech about one of her favorite subjects. "Coffee is absolutely ancient. See, it says on the package here: *First discovered by a man named Dhabhani on a trip to Ethiopia. There he enjoyed a greatly popular beverage – qahwa - which was flavorful and gave him a sense of renewed energy. He brought it back to his home in Yemen and his devout religious group appreciated how it helped them continue their long hours of prayers.*

"You see," she said looking up, "it gives you energy. Now, listen to this. *'Coffee houses were set up all around the Arab world, and eventually the habit spread to Europe and beyond. In the mid 1600's, England became a major importer of coffee, and coffeehouses flourished there.'* Now this is unbelievable. You still listening?"

Gittel nodded, so Sarah continued. *"Much of the American Revolution was planned in coffee houses far across the Atlantic by Paul Revere and others. After the Boston Tea Party, coffee became the favorite of Americans.* You see, it's downright patriotic to drink coffee."

"Well, that's nice," said Gittel, "but I really…"

"Watch this," said Sarah. She took a teaspoon size scoop and poured it into a mug, then filled it with boiling water. "Here's for me, and," she said as she poured a second cup, "here's for you. Now we add sugar. You can add as much as you want. I always take two spoons."

"I guess two spoons sounds good to me, too," said Gittel hesitantly.

"And we add milk," said Sarah, taking some fresh milk from the fridge and adding some to each cup. "Now, to really make this first cup of yours a special treat, we add a donut to the side." She took a package of donuts, and balancing their cups, the girls walked back to the dining room.

"You sure this is healthy?" asked Gittel.

"Hold on," said Sarah. She returned to the kitchen, came back with the jar, and held it out to Gittel. "You see any health warnings?"

Gittel turned the jar around in her hands and shrugged. "Well… not really."

"See. If it were unhealthy, the government would make them write it on the jar, like the warnings they print on wine labels, or the surgeon general's warning on a box of cigarettes. No, my friend. Perfectly safe. Perfectly good. Perfectly effective. And absolutely delicious."

After her cup of coffee, and donut, Gittel noticed that her brain seemed exceptionally sharp. Where a mere fifteen minutes ago, she had felt that the day was over, now she felt like it was beginning again. Suddenly, the connection between green eyes and earth was abundantly clear. Page after page of notes flipped through her nimble fingers. When she began to feel tired again around midnight, Sarah made her another cup of coffee. And at 2:00 AM, Gittel easily agreed with Sarah that it would be a great time to get a jump start on the American History for the following week.

At 3:00, when the last of Sarah's siblings turned off their bedroom light, and Sarah's mother called from her job at the hospital to remind them to lock the door before they went to sleep, they decided to call the night a day, and close their books.

As Gittel lay in the bed next to Sarah's, she had a hard time falling asleep. She tossed and turned, and kicked her feet. "My, but that coffee is magic, isn't it?" she said, as she tried to get comfortable in the unfamiliar bed. "I guess I've discovered the secret to finding more time at last. Who needs to sleep so much? Finally, I'll be able to burn the candle at both ends!" And she fell into a restless sleep.

The next morning, she started her day with a cup of coffee at Sarah's house, and then went to school to take her final. But she was no longer afraid of finals. She had a plan on how to get through the next two weeks of finals. It would be a breeze.

The following week, night after night, Gittel carried her heavy books home with her and studied. But she felt the pressure lifted. She didn't have to schedule her whole evening around studying. If she wanted to go to a wedding, she went, and then began studying afterwards. If she wanted to enjoy a home-made treat, she'd bake to her heart's delight, wait until it was cool from the oven, and then sit down to start. She covered *navi, halacha, tefilla,* with ease. True, each covered a year's worth of material, with pages of notes to read, but with more hours than she ever dreamed would be available, there was time for everything.

The next week was reserved for Hebrew language, and Jewish History, two of the subjects with the most details to memorize and review. Even Sarah was complaining about the workload.

"How will we ever get though all this?" she asked.

"Why do you complain so much?" Gittel had retorted. "It's easy if you have the time."

She studied practically all night for the Hebrew language test. She did notice that the more facts she shoved in to her brain, the more seemed to fly out, but it was probably the material, which seemed somewhat befuddling. As she worked, memorizing more and more translations, conjugations, and dots and dashes and frills, she hummed,

No need to sleep.
No need to stop.
Just study, study, study
'til you drop, drop, drop.

It was the night before the last final: Jewish History. Gittel sat down to study by herself, since Sarah had told her, in the first fight of their lives, that she was acting too aggressive and too pushy. "I mean, what's the fun of studying together, if you have to be so bossy about it?"

Gittel didn't care. She had discovered the secret to taking finals, and she would never give it up. Every hour or so, she drank another cup of coffee, each cup darker, and more full of caffeine than the one before it. She realized that her hands did seem to shake a bit as she filled in the practice test, but at that point, who cared? Her mother accused her of being nervous, her brother called her outright hostile, but what did it matter? They didn't understand. She was on a roll.

For two weeks now, she trained herself to sleep less than three hours a night, only making up some time on Shabbos. Each night she slept less and less, until she no longer had to dream of a day with 68 or 113 hours. Finally, she was able to maximize all 24 hours of the day she did have. Tonight, she had no plans of sleeping at all. She didn't need to -- with her coffee mug at her side.

The next morning, she got to school a little early, sleepless. As she stood in the hall, sipping a coffee she had brought from home, she felt her heart pounding against her chest. "I wonder what's wrong with me," she thought out loud. "I'm not nervous about the test. Not with the way I studied last night."

"Gittel, are you okay?" asked Sarah when she saw her in the hallway. "You look kind of jittery. Like, why are your eyes so red?"

"Whatever...It's nothing," Gittel said curtly. "I'm fine." She shrugged and pushed past her friend. "I'm fine, I said. Well, maybe a little dizzy, but I just want to finish this test, and collapse into…"

"*GITTEL!*" screeched Sarah as Gittel suddenly fell against the wall and slid down to the floor. Her hot drink splashed against the doorway, drowning her feet in a pool of coffee.

★★★

The next year, at the first-day-of-school assembly, school rules were handed out in neatly stapled packets to eager girls, dressed in brand new uniforms. There, on the last page, was a new rule. Sarah was the first to see it, and point it out to Gittel, sitting next to her.

"Wow!" Sarah whispered, "we're famous!"

And Gittel read: *"As of this year, we are instituting the new Sarah-Gittel rule, named for two students who learned this important lesson the hard way. This rule is in effect all year, but particularly during finals and during concert.*

Girls must guard their sleep schedules. Naturally we understand that people are different, and one rule will not suit all girls. However, there is no reason why a girl should not get 7-10 hours of sleep a night. This allows for both night owls and morning larks to sleep their choice of hours during the course of the night. Sleeping around the clock on Shabbos (known as 'sleeping a bagel') is not an acceptable replacement.

Your homeroom teacher will ask you to fill in a sheet each day during finals, stating the time you went to sleep and the time you woke up.

If a girl has not treated herself to a good night's sleep (because that's one of the biggest gifts you can give yourself!), she will be excused from class, with no questions asked, to go home and catch up on her sleep, and will be allowed to take a make up test during a make-up week following finals.

If it happens more than twice, she will be asked to speak with a school counselor for help with time management. For your own health, and the health of your friends, we ask you to abide by this new rule.

Enjoy your studies.

Gittel broke out in a grin. "They care," she said with tears in her eyes.

Sarah looked carefully at the rules again. "You know, they didn't say we're not allowed to drink coffee."

Gittel 'shuddered. "From now on, I'll stick to coffee ice-cream!"

Carlos

YOSSI AND ELI STOOD IN THE HALLWAY. Not that it was their choice. Rabbi Stein had made it quite clear that if they couldn't be quiet during Thursday's weekly *parsha* quiz, they would be asked to leave the classroom, and take the quiz after school.

"We weren't really talking," Yossi complained to Eli as the *rebbi* closed the door behind them.

"I know it. I just asked you for an eraser," Eli grumbled. "By mistake, I wrote that *Yisro* had six names, and then I remembered the seventh."

"He didn't have to kick us out of class for that, even though I asked you what that seventh name was."

"Yeah. If Yisro knew how much we were suffering, I think he would have just dropped a name," Eli sighed.

The two depressed boys shifted quietly from one foot to the other. They weren't used to being punished. Even seeing their own names on the honor roll of the bright bulletin board that decorated the hallway couldn't cheer their gloomy mood as they pondered the mess they had gotten into.

Yossi sighed and fidgeted. Eli leaned motionless against the wall, moving out of the way only to allow Carlos, the janitor, access to the spot as he slowly made his way down the hallway, past their fourth grade classroom, sweeping up the stray wrappers left on the floor during recess.

Yossi looked at the round clock that hung over the classroom door. "We're going to miss the bus," he groaned. "Plus, it started snowing during recess. How am I going to walk home without boots?"

"I hate Rabbi Stein," Eli said.

"Me too," Yossi agreed. "He's so mean."

Suddenly, Carlos stopped sweeping and turned on the boys. "What'd you say?" he growled, backing up and standing in front of the two boys. He leaned his broom on the wall and stood glowering over them, his thick, dark arms crossed on his chest.

"Nothin'," shrugged Yossi.

"It's just that we hate our teacher for making us stay after school," Eli added.

"Hey, man. That there is *loshon horo*. You gotta be careful in this here yeshiva not to say no *loshon horo*, man." His bright, white teeth flashed, and he picked up his broom and continued down the hall.

Eli laughed. "Hey, Carlos," he said. "You wanna sing us a song while you work?"

Carlos turned around seriously. "Hey, man. I don't sing no songs for boys who talk *loshon horo*." Then he chuckled, turned, and started whistling as he swept around the corner.

"That's the tune to the song '*shelo asani goy*,'" Eli explained. "My older brothers taught him that song when he first started working in yeshiva ten years ago."

"They taught him to sing about being thankful that he wasn't a *goy*? That's ridiculous," Yossi chuckled.

"Yeah. Cracks me up," Eli said. "But believe me, I've seen Carlos around town after hours. He must live somewhere close to my neighborhood because I see him driving his pick-up truck really fast up our street. And I've seen him drinking at that bar at the corner of our block. Looks to me like he's plenty happy to be a *goy*."

The door to the classroom opened, and Rabbi Stein's serious face met their smiles. "I didn't send you out here to have a party," he said. "The quiz is over. You may go quietly to your seats."

The boys went obediently, hoping it might make a difference in how they were treated after school.

But it didn't. They sat in their seats as their lucky classmates were dismissed, and then they were put in separate corners to complete the test. "Next week," Rabbi Stein said as he collected their papers and marked them each with a red "minus five" before even reading the answers, "I expect better behavior from my two star students."

Eli and Yossi hung their heads.

"Now," Rabbi Stein continued, "do you boys need a ride home? Your misbehavior doesn't absolve me from doing a *chesed* for a fellow Jew, does it?" he asked with a twinkle in his eye.

"Uh... sure! Thanks!" said Yossi. "And we live across the street from each other."

"And we're sorry," Eli added, feeling extreme regret for their former hatred of a man who could be so kind.

In the parking lot, they passed Carlos, who was fiddling with his pick-up truck in the cold air. "Good night, Carlos," Rabbi Stein replied.

"G'Night, Rabbi," Carlos replied, saluting. "An' good *Shabbos*."

"Good *Shabbos*?" Yossi laughed. "Today's Thursday."

"Blizzard," Carlos stated, peering up at the sky. "Ain't gonna be no school tomorrow. I got my plow here to attach to my truck. I think me an' my son Jose are gonna have some work to do this weekend."

"Then good Shabbos to you, too," Yossi and Eli said as they climbed into Rabbi Stein's warm car.

Carlos was right. It snowed all day Friday, and all of Shabbos. As soon as Shabbos was over, Eli got dressed in his warmest outdoor clothing -- including snowpants, extra thick socks, and sub-arctic gloves -- and rushed outside to meet Yossi. Fresh flakes continued to fly heavily downward. Alternate side of the street parking was cancelled and the snow covered the cars that were lined up and down the block, providing high banks of snow that concealed one side of the street from the other. Traffic was non-existent, except for the distant, muffled sound of an army of plows, beginning what would be a long night of clearing and pushing the heavy deposits of the sloppy storm. This was a night to remember.

Eli bent down, grabbed a handful of snow, formed a neat snowball with his waterproof gloves, and pitched it across the street.

In a second, a high speed snowball was returned.

"Hey! Is that you, Yossi?"

"Sure," said Yossi, popping up from behind a car.

Sploosh. Eli hit him with a wet surprise.

"Youch!" Yossi threw four balls in rapid fire at his friend.

The two boys ran back and forth, pitching and catching. It didn't take more than a few moments for more neighborhood boy to join. Shmueli, Yitzi and Meir joined Yossi on one side of the street, and Yehuda, Elimelech, and Gershy joined Eli on the other side.

Snowballs were flying fast and furious. "This is great!" Eli cried with glee.

"This is the stickiest, best snow ever!" shouted Yossi as he pitched snowball after snowball across the street.

Their cheeks were hot with excitement. Fun was in the air. There were so many snowballs flying, the boys hardly knew who was on which team anymore. It seemed that all the boys on the avenue were out, shoveling, digging, and laughing – even the kids from the public school who lived in the apartment building at the corner. What had stared with Eli's first snowball after *havdala* had turned into a massive snow war!

Eli came over to Yossi's side of the street and together they quickly built a fort between the garbage bins. They loaded it up with piles of snowballs, and then began pelting the hidden enemy on the other side of the road.

"Whoa!" came an anonymous shout. "The guys in the fort are stocking up!"

For a few minutes, snowballs stopped flying. It was clear that the enemy was planning a huge counter attack. Yossi gathered snowballs as fast as he could. He could hear a snow plow coming down the block, and he just hoped that the huge plow wings would deposit a big mountain next to *their* side of the street when he arrived. In the meantime, Eli fortified the top of the mound that they were hidden behind and got ready for...

"Go!" someone from the other side of the street shouted.

Instantly, some tens of snowballs flew in their direction. Yossi covered his head and Eli ducked down low until the rain subsided, and then Yossi stood up to deliver the counter attack.

At that minute, another snowball came flying – right into Yossi's head.

"OW! That was no snowball!" Yossi screamed.

"Hey! You can't put rocks inside!" Eli yelled. "That's not fair!"

"Yeah! I'm bleeding!" Yossi cried.

"Who said it's not fair?" shouted the voice from across the street. Another snowball was shot in Eli's direction. He ducked... and then gulped when he heard it crash into the metal garbage can with a loud clang.

"What's with the rocks?" Eli cried out in fear. "Shmueli, Yitzi, Meir ?! Why are you doing that?"

"Yehuda, Elimelech, Gershy!" Yossi continued. "Anyone out there?"

"Shmueli, Yitzi..." mimicked the voice. "Gershy... Judah...Judah... Judah..."

"They must have seen these guys coming and gone inside,"

Eli said nervously to Yossi. "What should we do now?"

Eli gasped. "We'd better get out of here!"

"How're we gonna make it home?" Yossi worried. "The enemy is invisible!"

"Should we run for it?"

"Home is at least fifty yards away," Yossi said miserably.

Suddenly, they heard the plow turn the corner. "This is our lucky break!" Yossi choked. "When he gets close, let's use him as a shield and try to make it home."

"Great plan," Eli said, "except it doesn't look like the enemy is going to wait until the plow comes." He threw himself onto the cold pile of snow inside their fort as a dozen rocks disguised as snowballs flew over his head and crashed into the trash cans.

The truck came closer... "Let's make a dash!" yelled Yossi.

Under a hail of stones and snowballs, Yossi and Eli covered their heads and tried to run home. Their hearts were beating so loudly, they barely heard the scrape of the snowplow right next to them. The next thing they knew, the plow suddenly skidded to a stop and the door banged open. Eli and Yossi froze in their places, hiding behind the tall snow tires.

"I'm gonna call the police right now if you guys ain't all off the street by the time I count to two!" raged a loud voice. "An' I'm already up to one an' a half!"

Feet pounded in the silence of the night. In a moment, the street was silent. Once more, soft flakes of snow continuing to drift beautifully downward, oblivious to the drama.

Yossi and Eli caught their breaths and emerged from behind the parked car to thank none other than their own Carlos, driving his pick-up truck-turned-plow.

"You saved us!" Yossi cried.

"They weren't playing fair!" Eli cried, allowing a tear of fright to finally trickle down his cheek in the darkness.

"Yeah, you guys was goners," Carlos said, shaking his head. "But ain't no one gonna throw rocks at my yeshiva boys when

Carlos is around," he said, the anger clear in his voice.

"I can't believe you stopped here just in time," Eli said, shaking.

"And you didn't even have to stop," said Yossi. "You could have just driven past a bunch of rowdy boys. I mean, when you opened the door, someone could have thrown a rock at you, too!"

"*Chas vashalom! Chas vashalom!*" Carlos said. "Neighbors gotta watch out for each other. And if it was my Jose stuck there like that, your daddy wouldn't a' done nothing different," Carlos said.

"I'm sure my father would like to thank you for rescuing us. We live right here. Would you like to come in and warm up?" Yossi asked. "And maybe have something to eat?"

Carlos hesitated by the side of his truck. "Ah – I don't wanna come in, man. I got work to do. But maybe you got a warm piece of kugel left over from Shabbos?"

"Sure!" said Yossi. "I'll pop it into the microwave and be right back." And he ran off.

Carlos turned to Eli. "And maybe you got some *choo-lent* too? The kind with *flanken*? Mmmm, mmm. That there is my very favorite Shabbos food."

"Sure," Eli said. "We always have way too much leftover after Shabbos. You can have all of it. Take some home to share with your Jose," he added generously, running off, and hoping that this week's Sunday night dinner might be pizza for a change.

Yossi and Eli returned in moments, and conveyed their parents appreciation and thanks. Then they passed the warm food through the front window of his truck.

"Hey, Carlos," said Yossi thoughtfully, leaning on the truck, "Did you ever think about becoming Jewish? You already know a lot more Torah laws than tons of American Jews."

"I know a whole lot of Tor-ah," Carlos laughed. "I hear them *yingalach* singin' all day long when I sweep them halls."

"And you're such a hero," Eli said. "You're really brave. I'll bet you'd make a very good Jew."

"Aint no way I'm gonna be Jewish, man," Carlos said, shaking his head. "I gotta have my bacon and eggs before I come to yeshiva every morning for *shakris*. But thanks for the Shabbos food." He climbed into his jeep. "You guys go ahead back home now and do your *parsha* sheets, and stay outta trouble. We don't need no frozen chosen people," he laughed as he popped the warm kugel into his mouth and drove off.

"Not every non-Jew is a *Yisro*," Yossi said as he said goodbye to Eli by his door.

"Not every one has to be," Eli responded. "But he's a really good *goy* to have around."

And Yossi whole heartedly agreed.

Boring

MITZI WAS HALF-DOZING ON THE COUCH in the middle of the afternoon, her arm dangling over the stuffed pillow at the end, her feet stretched across three seats, leaving only a tiny corner of the couch for Yaakov to squeeze into and savor the latest *frum* novel.

"What's it about, Yaakov?" she asked in a bored sort of voice, her eyes closed.

"Huh? Oh, Mitzi! It's great! You should feel my heartbeat!" His hands gripped the cover of the book. "I'm just up to where the enemy guards, who've been chasing the hero for at least six pages, finally tracked him down. See, they discovered him standing at the edge of a hundred foot mountain with the vultures circling above him in great, giant circles as the sole witnesses to...."

"Oh, brother. Sounds like a real cliff-hanger," she muttered. "I'm sorry I asked."

"So'm I," Yaakov muttered back, as he lost himself again in the pages of his book. The clocked ticked as Yaakov read and Mitzi snored.

"Mitzi! *Mitzi!*" Her mother appeared at the door to the living room wearing an exasperated expression. "I've been calling you for five minutes! Shiri just called me from Emuna Academy.

I have to run to run down to the school to give a hand with the flower sale, and Danny's playing outside. Can you just keep an ear open for him?"

"Um… sure…." Mitzi mumbled as turned over.

"Mitzi! Did you hear what I said?" her mother asked as she planted herself within ten inches of the couch and crossed her arms.

"Um… uh.. .what, Mommy? What is it?" Mitzi glanced up at her mother and noticed the exasperated look on her face.

"I said I'm going out and you have to watch Danny outside in the sandbox. Come on. Shake a leg. I'll be back in a half an hour."

Mitzi reluctantly lowered her feet to the floor, slipped on her shoes and went out to her big sisterly duties.

"Hi, boring Danny," she said as she sat down on the side of the wooden sandbox and flipped her long brown ponytail over her shoulder.

"Look!" he commanded, pointing.

"It's a truck, isn't it?" she yawned, seeing his yellow dump truck loaded with sand, leaning on its side.

"It crashed!" Danny told her. "Help me?"

Mitzi stood up and tipped the big truck over, dumping the sand back into the box.

"Great!" Danny exclaimed. Then he went to work with his plastic shovel, filling the truck back up again.

Mitzi groaned. How did Danny manage to keep so busy in this dumb box filled with sand? Every day he came out and played here, pushing the little grains back and forth, and around and around. Where was the fun? What held his interest in this four by four patch of backyard to the point that he would cry on rainy days when he missed sitting here, getting dirty, and pushing that sand around?

Mitzi looked up at the blue sky, dappled with fluffy white clouds. Another nice day. Another boringly nice day. Watching Danny was boring. This whole backyard was boring. The whole block where her family lived, which they and their neighbors prided themselves on being "so nice and quiet," was boring.

School was winding down for the year. The teachers, who in the beginning of the year had been unknown and exciting, were already as familiar as the old plaster walls. The thrill of entering high school had given way to the tedium of tests and quizzes that appeared as regularly as the changes in the traffic light outside the building. Even the art teacher, who came in one day with a big box of various mysterious tools to draw and the next day with colored papers, newsprint, ink and glue, had become predictable in her unpredictability. When had the September alertness given way to this end-of-the-year exhaustion?

Maybe it was the new high school friends she started associating with this year, the ones whose cool attitude she had admired and endeavored to emulate. She had learned to temper her excitement with a shrug, not to look too anxious, not to seem too interested. At first it had been an effort. Now she was as cool as the rest.

But being cool came with a price. When she got used to pouring cold water on any new idea, she built up an icy skin. And after that, not much could penetrate. Suddenly, everything at home, seemed repetitious -- the same as last year, and the year before.

At least her brother Tzvi had an exciting life. He was traveling out-of-town next week for *Shavuos*, all the way to Lonesville, where he and some friends would spend *Yom Tov* with people who were eager to learn Torah. Traveling might be fun, Mitzi sighed.

But what keeps everyone *else* so interested? Mitzi suddenly wondered. What keeps my parents so enthusiastic about Shabbos and *Yom Tov*, week after week and year after year? Why does old Mr. Gibbetz, the ninety year next-door neighbor, still hobble to *shul* on Tatty's arm, to hear the Torah *leining*? Isn't it the same *aseres hadibros* that they read last year in *shul*? He probably knows it all by heart!

Mitzi shook her head. At fourteen, she felt she had already done it all. Life at home was dull, dull, dull. Why couldn't her life be more like the novel that Yaakov was reading: fast-paced, and exciting?

★★★

The car door slammed. "Yaakov, Mitzi, Danny!" Mommy called, "come help with the boxes!"

Danny jumped out of the sandbox and ran to see what his mother and Shiri had brought home, while Mitzi followed slowly behind. Yaakov came out the front door, his nose still in his book. "Give a hand, kids," Mommy said as she lugged box after box of long, white boxes out of the car.

Yaakov quickly flipped to the last page. There. The hero's name still appeared in the last paragraph. Well, at least he would survive, Yaakov consoled himself, as he reluctantly set down the book and grabbed a box.

"You wouldn't believe what's going on in that school," Mommy puffed. "I was supposed to pick up these boxes of flowers and deliver them to the grocery store so they could set up a stand to sell flowers for the few days before *Shavuos*, but the air-conditioning is broken in the store. With weather like this, the owners are afraid to have such a huge stock of flowers wilting by their cash registers. Instead, Mrs. Ginsberg practically begged me to open up a flower store in our living room!"

"Whoopee," muttered Mitzi. "What a mess."

"Mitzi!" Mommy said, turning to her daughter with her eyes blazing. "This is for Emuna Academy! EA treats you and Shiri very well. This is the least we can do! Now come grab a box and *shlep* it into the living room. We're going to have to set the air conditioner to a colder temperature... and we'd better put some kind of mats on the carpets to protect them from the crowds. The sale starts tomorrow and ends on *Erev Shavuos*.."

Yaakov helped set up the tables in the living room in a large semi circle. Mitzi sighed and grabbed a box. As she and her siblings opened the boxes and arranged the flowers on the tables, the fresh fragrance of carnations, roses, lilies, and lilacs filled the room. Then Shiri and Mitzi arranged the flowers on the tables according to price, putting the fancy terrariums safely on the back table.

"Look at this," Shiri pointed. "There's a bee nestled inside of this bunch here."

"Good for him," Mitzi said. "I think we're almost done here, Mommy. Time to take a break."

But before Mitzi could excuse herself, Tatty came in *shlepping* a huge cardboard box that was stamped "EZ2 Build." "Whoa! What's going on here?" asked Tatty when he saw the flowers.

"Flower sale tomorrow," mumbled Mitzi from behind the table. "For school. Mommy took over."

"But where should I put the new bookshelf I just bought?" Tatty asked, measuring the room with his eye.

"New bookshelf?" Mommy asked. "Why do we need a new bookshelf?"

"For the new *seforim*, of course," explained Tatty, with a gleam in his eye. "You wouldn't believe it. I was browsing in the store for a new book for *Shavuos*, something to add a bit of inspiration, when I saw that they reprinted the entire series of *Teshuvas* from Rav Yosef, Rav Yehoshua, Rav Shmuel, and Rav Eliyahu! Thirty-six volumes in new, easy-to-see print, with footnotes and indexes. I just couldn't resist...."

"I guess the *seforim* will have to go in the dining room," Mommy answered from behind a flower arrangement. "Oh dear, there's another bee!" she said as she put down the vase on the table.

"I never saw so many bees!" Danny whined, hiding behind his mother.

"It's true," Mommy said thoughtfully. "And it's quite interesting. Did you know that across the United States and Europe, people are terribly worried about bees going extinct? It's a crisis, since bees pollinate flowers and plants. Without plants, there would be no animals, and without either one, people wouldn't be able to survive."

"Yes, I've read about it too," Tatty added. "They're calling it Colony Collapse Disorder. They're even importing bees from other countries. Don't kill any of these bees, kids. We need them."

"Yeah, right," mumbled Mitzi. "Guests for *Yom Tov*."

"Well, they work harder than you do," Shiri said, lifting a box of roses. "Give me a hand already. I want to get back to my spinach lasagna recipe for *Yom Tov*."

"I think we'll all be better off if you don't get back to that recipe." Mitzi said, annoyed. "Can't you pull the tablecloth down from your side so I can put down this heavy box?"

"Girls, there's lots to do, so I suggest we work together," Mommy said sternly. "Just give me a second to call the company that supplied us with the flowers. It really does seem that there are a lot of bees."

★★★

"Mitzi!"

Mitzi rolled over, yawned and realized the sun was already pretty high in the sky. It was *erev Yom Tov*, but she hadn't seen any real need to wake up early. Why were her parents calling her?

She pulled herself out of bed, washed *negel vasser*, got dressed, and came down to the kitchen. *Uh oh*, Mitzi thought to herself, *it's going to be a speech about attitude. I can feel it coming. Why aren't I helping with the flower sale? Why aren't I baking cheesecake? Why aren't I preparing a d'var Torah for the meal? Why don't I at least read an interesting book?* She knew she hadn't been very cooperative this week, but she really was not in the mood for *mussar*. She clenched her teeth, threw her ponytail over her shoulder, and slouched into the kitchen.

Her mother and father were both standing there, looking rather annoyed, but it didn't look like they were annoyed with *her*. In fact, if anything, it seemed like they wanted her help.

Mommy began. "Mitzi, I know you're tired from your hard work in school…"

"Well, um…" Mitzi looked down. She wasn't tired from working hard. She was just plain tired of everything.

"And I hate to impose too much on you…"

"But?" Mitzi didn't know what was coming, but it seemed like it was going to be a lot of work.

"But that Tzvi of ours missed his ride to Lonesville. You know how much the people are counting on him to lead some classes. Tatty was up most of the night, struggling to build his new book-shelf, and I was up organizing the flowers. If we leave now, one of us can drive there, and the other one can drive back, so we'll each get a chance to nap in the car. Do you think you can handle *erev Yom Tov* here on your own?"

Mitzi shrugged. "What's the big deal?"

"Great!" Mommy said. She was already in fast-motion, glancing at her watch, grabbing her pocketbook, and issuing instructions over her shoulder. "We should be home with plenty of time to spare before *Yom Tov*. Shiri's making the blintzes, and then she'll give Danny a bath. Yaakov will finish with the bookshelf and when the *seforim* are delivered, he'll load them onto the new shelves. All you have to do is sit by the flower tables and take money from people. It'll probably be a slow day for the business, and by four o'clock you be able to close up shop and get ready for *Yom Tov*. Tatty, you have the keys? Let's go, Tzvi! Bye!"

And they were gone in a proverbial cloud of dust. Mitzi sat down by the table. *Ho- hum.* She could smell the blintzes from the kitchen. Shiri must have been up hours ago. She could hear Danny, shoveling the sand in his sandbox. Yaakov was hammering away in the dining room. She sighed, and stretched over to the end table to reach a *siddur* to begin *davening,* but was interrupted by a knock at the door. Customers already?

She got up to open the door. "Hello?"

The man on the door step was wearing an ID card on his

pocket. "Mr. Press here," he said. "I'm a reporter for the science section of the National News Journal. Ever see our paper?"

"Uh, sorry. I'm kind of not that interested in science," Mitzi said with a semi-scowl.

"The flower supplier sent me to observe the bees that have come to your little flower sale here and send them a scientific report. It's quite an interesting phenomenon…" With that, he stepped past her and moved slowly between the flower tables, examining the varieties of displays, and stopping briefly to enter notes in his laptop.

Mitzi shrugged and went to pick up her *siddur,* but the doorbell rang again. "So much for a quiet day," she grimaced as she opened the door to allow a gaggle of women to enter.

"I just popped by to see how you were managing," said Mrs. Ginsberg.

"Oh, we're so happy you're open," said Mrs. Zee.

"I don't know why we left buying flowers for the last minute," said Mrs. Cee.

"A bee!" said little Zisi Cee, pointing to an arrangement of roses.

"Yes," said Mr. Press. "It seems there's an abundance of bees on this shipment of flowers. If you don't bother them, though, they generally won't bother you."

It took only moments before all the people in the living room were best of friends. For over two hours, the crowd grew. Mrs. Swiller edged her way in with her darling triplets, and Mrs. Diller browsed around the tables, smelling each bouquet. The customers seemed interested in the reporter, and the reporter was just as intrigued with the customs of *Shavuos* and the flower buying as he was with the bees, and no one seemed to be in a rush. Mitzi snuck away to *daven* quickly and then did her best to move the traffic along, quoting prices, taking money and giving change.

There was a shrill ring of the phone. "Hey, Mitzi!" Shiri called from the kitchen. "I'm up to my elbows in cheese filling for the blintzes. Can you get it?"

"Got it! Oh, hi, Tzvi, my far away brother!" Mitzi answered, trying to keep the jealousy out of her voice. "You arrived safe and sound? How's it going over there?"

"Can't hear you, Mitz. What's all the noise there?"

Mitzi moved to the corner of the room with the phone. "Is this better? It's Mommy's flower sale. The company that sent the flowers here sent down a reporter who's trying to get the story of why there are so many bees here. How's it there?" she asked. "Meet any new people? See any new sights?"

Suddenly there was a loud crash from the living room.

"What was *that* noise?"

"Oh, whatever. I think it's the new bookshelf that Tatty was trying to build and Yaakov took over. One second, Tzvi…. The roses are $14.50; the daffodils are $12. No, I have no idea which will live longer… Hey Tzvi, you still there? Tatty and Mommy are already on their way back? Okay... Have a great *Yom Tov*, Tzvi. Think of us, back here in Dullsville."

She hung up before she heard Tzvi reply, "Doesn't sound so dull to me…"

When Mitzi picked up the next bunch of daisies, to hand them to Mrs. Swiller, she noticed three bees were flying around.

"Hey, Mr. Press," Mrs. Swiller said as she poked around in her pocket book for money, "this bunch might interest you. It seems to be loaded…"

"I'm sorry about that," Mitzi said, and she waved her hand to get rid of the bees.

But the bees seemed not to want to move. If anything, they seemed more and more agitated as people crowded around to see them. Without warning, one of the bees flew straight for Mitzi and stung her on the neck.

"OW!" she screamed.

"Oh dear," said Mrs. Swiller.

"Get some toothpaste," said Mrs. Zee.

"Salt," suggested Mrs. Cee.

"Maybe baking soda?" said Diller.

"Put on some garlic. Or was it onion?" Mrs. Ginsberg offered.

"Ahem," said the science reporter. "Step one: remove the stinger. Here let me." He pulled the stinger out quickly, wrapped the sharp, saw-edged needle in a tissue, and stuck it in his jacket pocket. "Necks are terrible places for bites, but of course, they didn't ask you. Step two: a cold compress is probably the best treatment."

"Shiri!" Mitzi called to the kitchen, "can you get me a..."

Suddenly, Mitzi stared coughing. "What in the world..." she said, as she tried to take a deep breath. "My tongue feels so swollen... Uch. I don't feel so good, but," she clenched her teeth together, "there is no *way* I'm going to throw up with so many people here! But... gasp...I... I.. can't breath!"

Shiri ran in with the cold compress, but Mr. Press was already running out to his car, leaping over boxes of flowers and throwing open his car door. He was back in seconds with a briefcase, which he flicked open. "Never research bees without an Epi-pen handy. This is an emergency," he said clearly to all the flower customers. "Anaphylactic reaction to a bee sting. Move back, folks," he said as he coolly jabbed the shot into Mitzi's leg.

Some of the by-standers pushed forward to see, others pushed back to get out of the way. The smell of burning blintzes filtered in from the kitchen and the smoke detector began to blare. At that minute, Danny decided to march in with his dump truck, leaving a trail of sand behind him. And, in the midst of the mayhem, the doorbell rang once again, and a UPS man started unloading boxes of books.

"Signature anyone?" he shouted over the commotion.

Mrs. Swiller signed for the books as Mitzi's breathing returned to normal.

"I have a pounding headache," she said to Mr. Press.

"I'm not surprised," he replied. "So do I. Let's get you out into the air." They stood on the front steps while Shiri took over wrapping up the flower business.

"You're going to have to go to a doctor just to get checked over," Mr. Press said. "And I hope you have other career plans for your future besides being a flower girl. Did you *know* you're allergic to bees?""

Mitzi managed a weak smile. "It's the first time I was ever stung. I guess now I know."

"That was a close one," Mr. Press continued as he packed up his briefcase. "It's rare that a first sting produces such a reaction. Only 2% of the population is really allergic to bee stings, even though most people do find them painful. You'll have to carry an Epi-pen with you from now on, like all people who are severely allergic to bees. In fact," he said slowly, turning pale, "I believe I saved your life." He gulped, and sat down suddenly on the front steps, his hands shaking. "Give me a second to get over this."

"Shiri! Bring that cold compress!" called Mitzi. "I think Mr. Press is going to faint!"

★★★

Later on, as she cleaned up the living room, Mitzi thought back on the week. She had been lulled into believing that life was tedious. She refused to catch her mother's enthusiasm about helping the school, or be infected by her father's excitement about the new *seforim* he was purchasing. She looked down on Yaakov's thrill over a new book, and certainly on Danny's fascination with the sandbox . She even refused to get involved in Shiri's love of good food, of cooking, and of baking for *Yom Tov*. Everyone else in the family had their own way of enjoying life.

And Mitzi?

It took a bee sting to wake her up to the intense joy of being alive. Life itself was pretty exciting, she suddenly realized. All she had to do to enjoy every day was focus on things that mattered to her, to wake up and smell the flowers – when there weren't any bees around, of course.

An hour before *Yom Tov*, the last leaves were gathered into garbage bags, the sand was swept out of the house, the books were arranged like soldiers on the new bookcase, and the table was set. Mrs. Ginsberg had stopped by from Emuna Academy with a huge cheesecake to thank Mommy for all her efforts on behalf of the school. Since they already had a cheesecake that Shiri had baked, Mommy quickly wrote a fresh card and sent the cake to Mr. Press's house, with a flowery thank you note for saving her daughter's life.

Finally, by the time Mommy benched *licht*, all was back in order.

"Mitzi," Mommy sighed after Kiddush, "I'm sorry we don't have any company for this *Yom Tov*. I know you would have liked a bit of excitement. We usually try to have some guests to liven up the meals, but with the flower sale, and the book delivery and the last minute trip to Lonesville, and the trip to the doctor, I'm afraid it's going to be a quiet, boring *Yom Tov*."

"Boring is kind of nice," Mitzi smiled weakly rubbing her neck.

"I still wonder why our flowers were covered with bees," Tatty said. "Did Mr. Press reach any conclusions?"

Yaakov shrugged. Danny reached for the butter to cover his *challa* for a *Shavuos* treat. Shiri got up to serve her home made blintzes.

"I wonder," Mommy said as she took a bite of salmon.

But Mitzi didn't need Mr. Press to tell her why the bees had come. They had come for her, to wake her up just in time to have a meaningful *Shavuos*.

The Class
No One Could Teach

NAFTOLI PRESSED HIMSELF TO THE WALL outside the door marked "Rabbi Rosenthal, Principal," and listened. Inside the office, the voices rose and fell as he stood, hardly breathing. Then, just as a hand was placed on the inner handle of the door, Naftoli slithered as fast as he could out to the hall and back toward his classroom. He broke into a run as he heard Rabbi Luzer's last sentence echo down the hall: "And good luck finding someone else to take over that class!"

"Our spy is back!" announced Yitz, as Naftoli returned from his mission.

"Whad'ya hear?"

"Whad'they say?"

"What happened?" asked a chorus of voices.

"He's out," answered Naftoli with a smirk.

The class erupted in a volcano of noise, the sounds bouncing off the walls.

"Yippee!"

"Another one falls!"

"That's number five this year!"

"And counting!" someone added.

The wild noise and boisterous hoots would have gone on for

a long time, if not for the sudden entry of Rabbi Rosenthal. One look -- and the boys meekly returned to their seats. He stood in the doorway, folded his arms, in his inimitable way, and stared around the classroom over the rim of his glasses until the class was back in control.

"Another apology note, I'll bet," whispered Yitz to Naftoli.

"I could write it in my sleep," replied Naftoli.

"Silence," demanded Rabbi Rosenthal. Yitz watched as the principal very slowly walked to the front of the room, and stood facing the boys. After eight years of having Rabbi Rosenthal as his principal, Yitz knew better than to argue when he had *that* look on his face.

Rabbi Rosenthal shook his head. Why couldn't he get this class to conform? How would these boys be accepted into high schools? Didn't they realize their reputations were at stake? What went wrong?

"What went wrong?" he asked, thinking out loud. That was his style: Open and frank. "So, let me hear, boys. What went wrong? Why did Rabbi Luzer just leave, in the middle of the day, promising never to set foot in this classroom again?"

He waited. Many boys shifted nervously in their seats. Yitz looked down at the pencil he twirled between his fingers. Five more minutes, and it would be lunch time. Then he would get the play by play story from Naftoli on the latest teacher's quitting speech that he heard from behind the office door.

As Rabbi Rosenthal asked his probing questions, Yitz actually found himself wondering what the answers could be. What *did* go wrong? Why *couldn't* the boys behave? Didn't they have any respect?

What went wrong was that he knew that he was smarter than the teacher, and he lost no time in sharing this fact with the rest of the class. The boys didn't behave because they didn't respect the teacher. Long ago, when they were small, and the teacher was, frankly, large, they followed their *rebbis* like little ducklings, out to the park, back to the class, to the lunchroom.

He could still remember exactly what Rabbi Sneider had for breakfast every day – kasha with cottage cheese – because throughout the entire third grade, Yitz insisted on eating the same thing. Back then, teachers were different.

What went wrong with Rabbi Luzer? Yitz almost guffawed aloud. Half the class was at least as tall as Rabbi Luzer, and far smarter. The man couldn't work a computer, or figure out how to program a cell phone. He still handed out hand written stencils, and wore the dullest suits. Yesterday, Rabbi Luzer came in with a sheet of questions to answer on the *parsha*. Yitz had convinced all the boys in advance to fill in the blanks with words from *Ashrei* and *Aleinu* so that the tests would look filled in. Today, they weren't surprised by the scolding and departure of their teacher.

After all these years, Yitz considered himself an expert on teachers. He read all the parenting and *chinuch* columns in the newspaper, and knew exactly how teachers should motivate their students and control the class. If it would be up to him, teachers would be voted in to their positions. Yes—that was a great idea. This was a democratic country. The school should hold an open democratic election, Yitz decided. Let the students choose who they would like to learn from, and the teachers who couldn't win the students over didn't belong in front of the class. He could just imagine the teachers lining the halls with signs and placards: *Vote for me! I'll give you more recess! I promise you more trips! I'll never give homework, or tests, or quizzes.* Ah! That would be the kind of school he would enjoy. Yitz smiled at his innovative idea, and even chuckled to himself.

"Yitzchok, is there something you'd like to share with us?" Rabbi Rosenthal's stern voice broke into his daydream.

Yitz shook his head. It just didn't pay to start up with Rabbi Rosenthal, even though Yitz was sure he was smarter than the principal. Yitz put on his serious, attentive face.

"As I said," Rabbi Rosenthal continued, "you boys have been

the cause of the fifth teacher this year quitting. I'm very disappointed. At this point, in the spring, with only a bit more than a month left of school, it will be impossible to find a teacher. If you cannot treat a teacher properly, you will have to learn without the one.

"Therefore, I am moving your class into the computer lab. Each day, you will listen on the headphones to a prepared *shiur*, follow along on the screen, and answer the questions. You'll take turns once a week presenting the material you've learned to your classmates. There will be a final exam on the material, which you will have to pass in order to graduate.

"You have earned yourselves a title: The Class No One Could Teach. I hope you're proud of yourselves," he finished, his voice dripping with sarcasm.

The boys silently rose, wearing serious looks. Rabbi Rosenthal turned and left the room, just as the bell rang for lunch.

Without prompting, Naftoli stood by the door and peeked down the hallway. As soon as he saw Rabbi Rosenthal enter his office, he turned back to his classmates and gave them a thumbs up. The silence was broken by a whoop and a cheer.

"We did it!"

"We're smarter than all the teachers in the school!"

"Smarter than all the teachers in the world!"

"Computers every day instead of once a week!"

No more teachers? Yitz's face had an incredulous look. *We're free!*

★★★

The next day, Yitz sat by his computer, along with the rest of his classmates. After being shown how to click into the programs they needed, each boy set off at his own pace. Yitz concentrated on the material in front of him. *Kind of nice, to be one-on-one with a machine that moves as fast as I want.* He peeked over at Naftoli's screen. Naftoli was two pages behind. Other boys were even doing different subjects. One boy chose to do *chumash* first; another flitted back and forth between *gemara* and *navi*.

The class was much quieter than it had been in a long time. The fact that the computer lab was directly opposite the principal's office was a big factor, but there was also the fact that each boy was directly responsible for his own learning. There was no snoozing in the back of the class, or *shmoozing* in the aisles. Each boy had to pull his own weight. Plus, on some level, they wanted to prove they were right – that learning could happen without teachers.

Yitz was sure it could.

At lunch, as the boys stood in line to wash, they compared notes.

"Where'd you get up to?" Zalmy asked Yitz.

"I'm holding in the third *perek*. How about you?"

"Well, I got a little stuck in the second *perek,* and I just kept reading the same words over and over. Finally, I just changed subjects. Do you think you can explain the Rashi at the top of the page to me?"

Yitz thought. "I think I skipped that one. Maybe Shlomo can help…" Shlomo was always good at catching on to difficult subjects. "Hey! Shlomo—did you get that Rashi in the second *perek*?"

"Second *perek* of what? I was learning *Halacha*. I spent the morning learning about how to wash before a meal. Just in time for lunch," he added. "See, you've got to dry your hands first *before* you wash with a cup." Shlomo made a show, wiping his hands on his pants, to demonstrate his new-found knowledge.

Meir piped up. "I opened the *Halacha* program first, too. The only thing is, in my house, my father doesn't say the *bracha* before he dries his hands. He says the *bracha* while he's drying them. Now I'm not sure what to do, and I don't know whether all the other things I studied this morning are right, either."

No one verbalized the obvious thought. If they had a teacher, he would be able to tell them what the *Halacha* was, why some people have one way of acting, and some another. And, he'd be able to explain that Rashi in the second *perek*… or at least find someone who could.

Still, day after day, Yitz was incredibly covering more ground than he ever dreamed possible. He made one *siyum* after the next, albeit alone at home with his family. He took the tests that the principal prepared, and did quite well on learning the facts, and figures, measurements and material. He went overboard to prove that he was indeed the most brilliant boy that had ever passed through the doors of his school.

One day, as the boys were learning, they heard a racket in the hallway. Naftoli was at the door to the computer lab before anyone else, and listened to the conversations in the halls. A few minutes later, he was back in his seat, tapping at the computer keys.

"What's up, Naftoli?" called Yitz from his computer across the room.

"The *schach* is up on the *sukka* in the *mishna*. I'm just not sure how high the *sukka* is allowed to be." Naftoli replied.

"Come on! I mean, what's up in the halls?"

"Yeah, that's your job, Naftoli," insisted Shlomo. "What's going on?"

"Nothing," Naftoli shrugged.

A second later, loud voices echoed upwards through the open windows of the computer lab. Shlomo, Zalman and a handful of other boys rushed to see what was the ruckus, but they also returned to their seats, and continued their work in a begrudging way.

What is going on here? Yitz wondered. *Why doesn't anyone want to talk?*

Yitz didn't want to appear too curious. He waited a few minutes, then made a show of coughing and got up to get a drink. On his way, he passed the windows, just in time to see seven busses pull out of the parking lot. The rest of the school was on the way to a Lag B'Omer trip.

With their teachers.

Yitz forgot about his drink, and sat back down by his computer, with the same expression he had seen on his classmates' faces. *Next file, next screen, click, and double click. Sigh. You couldn't go on a* lag ba'omer *trip with a dumb old machine.*

★★★

One day, Yitz noticed that Shlomo didn't come to Yeshiva. He didn't come the next day either. A week went by. Rumors swirled around the class. Some kids said he moved, some kids said he was too sick to come, but even the sickness had different names, depending on which kid you asked. Boys tried calling, but Shlomo was never "available." It seemed there was a huge cover-up going on in Shlomo's house.

After another week went by, the boys got more and more concerned. "Fourteen year old boys just don't drop off the face of the earth," insisted Naftoli. "Something must have happened to him."

"If he's sick, we'll all pitch in and say *Tehilim…*" Zalman added.

"I can't believe he would move without saying good-bye," said Meir with a frown.

Finally, Yitz made up his mind that he would get the truth straight from the source. *I'm not scared of asking, and I'm not scared of his parents. If it's something private, I'll leave him alone, but shouldn't someone check him out?!* Yitz thought.

And, so, armed with determination, Yitz marched up to Shlomo's door at 6:00 in the evening, and knocked loudly. *There are lights on. At least someone still lives here,* he thought.

The door was opened by none other than Shlomo himself, looking entirely well, and not at all troubled, sick, or otherwise excusable from school, with an ice-cream in one hand and a *sefer* in the other.

"Hi Shlomo," Yitz said hesitantly.

"Hi," said Shlomo, with a noncommittal tone, as if it were the most natural thing in the world to be home for the evening, chomping on an ice-cream cone, after skipping two weeks of school.

"Uh… I'm the truant office," said Yitz, with a slight smile. "I was sent here because there have been reports that someone in this household hasn't been attending school."

"Who?" asked Shlomo, and then he caught himself, and looked down. "I guess you mean me."

"Well, yeah," said Yitz. "Someone noticed that your computer wasn't turned on in the last two weeks. We just wanted to make sure you're still alive, that's all."

"Yeah, I'm alive alright, *baruch Hashem.*"

Silence.

"Hey, Shlomo! Stop playing games. What's goin' on? Where've you been? I mean, if you don't want to talk, I'll just go away, but there's a lot of people wondering what's become of you."

Shlomo sighed. "I guess I can't keep it a secret forever. My parents didn't go for the new set up in school. They went down to Rabbi Rosenthal's office a bunch of times, but he insisted that there was nothing he could do… They're worried about me being accepted into a *mesivta* if I would be part of 'The Class That No One Could Teach.' So two weeks ago they switched me to Yeshiva Darchei Avos."

Yeshiva Darchei Avos! They had always been the competition! Yitz shrugged as if it didn't matter. "Well, good luck sitting in old, boring class again… obeying all those rules, raising your hand when you need a drink, and all that."

"Hey. Don't get insulted, Yitz."

"Oh, I don't care. You're probably just plodding on with one *posuk* at a time. I wish I could hang around and eat ice-cream with you, but I've got to go now, Shlomo. I have sixteen *perakim* of *navi* to review before the test tomorrow, and Zalman's waiting for me."

As Yitz turned a cold shoulder on his former friend and marched down the sidewalk, Shlomo called after him: "Enjoy Zalman while you have him! I heard his parents talking to mine last night on the phone. And Naftoli's parents called too, by the way. Within a few weeks, it might just be you and your computer left in that lab!" And Shlomo slammed the door.

★★★

The season of "*mesivta* decisions" had arrived. It came every year with the pollen, and settled over the country side like cherry blossoms on a spring day. Words flitted and flew - names, recommendations, news and gossip - like baby birds out on their first flight. With a bump and a jolt, decisions were made, rescinded, redecided, and then finally let out in the public air. It was the talk on the street and the talk in *shul*, the constant conversation among parents and boys: "*Where are you going to learn next year?*"

By this point, Yitz's class had shrunk considerably while Yeshiva Darchei Avos's eighth grade swelled. Each day when Yitz came into the lab, there was another computer with the off button pressed down, and another empty chair. In fact, as days turned to weeks, it looked like Shlomo had been correct. Yitz would be the sole graduate of his class.

And, somehow, each high school that Yitz applied to told his parents that coming year's class was already full, or the dorm couldn't accommodate another boy. One place wasn't giving final decisions until the end of the summer, but then it seemed that Zalman was accepted there the next week. Another one seemed to have a policy of only one boy from each elementary school, but then Shlomo and Naftoli both decided to go there for the coming year. Everyone had only compliments for Yitz's learning, and his accomplishments, but didn't seem to think that their school would be able to accommodate him.

And there was no one to intercede on his behalf. No one to turn to for advice. No one who had a connection to an old yeshiva who would call up and say "I know this boy, and I can guarantee he will be a fine *talmid* for your ninth grade." Like a man without a country, he was a boy without a teacher.

Yitz sat alone in front of his computer, truly confused. *What happened to my reputation? What went wrong? I wish the com-*

puter could write me a recommendation or call a Mesivta on my behalf! But the computer just sat on his desk, silent, waiting from commands from its operator.

Yitz shook himself. It wouldn't do to become too emotional about the whole thing. Since he didn't have a teacher this year, he would have to find an old teacher of his who would be willing to help him out; someone who could recommend the right yeshiva for him, and put in a good word. *I know! I'll go back and observe the other classes, and pick out my favorite rebbi to do the job.* Set on his mission, he immediately walked out of the computer lab and down the hall, peeking in each door along the way.

It was near the end of the year. The walls of the classrooms sported charts and pictures that the teachers had on display. Funny… the computer room had empty walls. No one to bother with decorating…

In first grade, the boys were *shuckling* and singing the *pasuk* they were learning. Suddenly, Yitz saw the *rebbi* jump on the chair and the children laughing with glee. Yitz still remembered the *rebbi* doing the same thing when he was in first grade to demonstrate how the angels on Yaakov's ladder went up and down. Hhhmmm…. No one acted out anything in the computer room.

In seventh grade, he noticed the *rebbi* demonstrating how to write on parchment with a quill. Each boy took a turn to write a letter by the teacher's desk. Yitz stopped to watch through the window. This very month, he had learned all the *halachos* on the computer, but he never even touched a quill… never really saw how dark black the ink was, or felt the soft, velvety parchment. No one in the computer room to help them understand *Halacha l'maaseh*, how to carry out the laws they learned…

And outside the fifth grade classroom, he saw a boy standing in the hall, deep in conversation with a *rebbi*. As they finished, he saw the *rebbi* put his arm around the boy's shoulder as he walked back to the class.

Yitz felt his heart constrict. That's what he was missing most of all. Someone who cared about him!

Suddenly Yitz felt a hand clamp down on *his* shoulder. It was Rabbi Rosenthal!

"My entire eighth grade is standing here in the hall," Rabbi Rosenthal stated with a grimace. "But it's good that you're here. Rabbi Tzviling's wife just called with an emergency with one of their twins and I have to drive him to the hospital. Can you stand in as a substitute for the fourth grade for just a few minutes until the real sub shows up?"

Yitz's eyes sparkled. "My pleasure." *At last, a chance to prove his superior talents. This would earn him a place in any mesivta.*

Rabbi Rosenthal hustled Rabbi Tzviling into the car, and Yitz confidently walked into the fourth grade.

"I see we're holding in *Parshas Vayishlach*," he began. "You -- in the first row…Read the next *pasuk*."

The boy ignored him.

Yitz stood over him. "I told you to read."

"Don't want to."

"What's your name?" Yitz asked, annoyed that the boy dared to defy him.

"Mr. Magoo," the boy replied, and then burst out in gales of giggles, while the rest of the class followed suit.

Within a few seconds, the class was on wheels, and Yitz was fighting for control. "Hey, sit down. Hey you, get off the chair. Put down that airplane. Get off his back. Stop spilling that juice. Hey! Get away from the window! I said *'get away from the window.'* SHOW A LITTLE RESPECT!" he finally screamed.

Suddenly, the class was silent. The boys hurried back and stood next to their seats. *Finally,* thought Yitz. "Ahem. Please sit down and let's go back to the *pasuk*…"

And then he realized it wasn't him they were standing up for. They were focused on someone behind him. The substitute had walked in the door.

Yitz turned, and found himself face to face with Rabbi Luzer.

***

"So, you want me to write you a letter of recommendation to a *mesivta*," said Rabbi Rosenthal. "Oh, dear. I'm afraid you're way to smart for any place that I can think of. None of the ninth grade *rebbis* would be brilliant enough for you to respect."

"He wouldn't have to be brilliant," Yitz insisted.

"Yes, but in one *mesivta*, the *rebbi* is rather old. He has an accent. You wouldn't like that. And in another, the *rebbi* speaks kind of quietly. And in the *mesivta* I was thinking of for you, the *rebbi* is just a nice fellow who likes kids and explains things very clearly… I don't think you'd go for that. You need someone who…."

"No, no," Yitz said. "I mean, I'm sorry for interrupting, but nice would be nice. I think that I could learn to respect anyone who has the guts to stand in front of a class day after day." He thought about his fourth grade fiasco and shuddered. "I guess every teacher deserves respect."

"Fine, then. I'll see what I can do to arrange an interview, and I'll put in a good word for you."

"Thank you," said Yitz humbly. "I guess I really don't deserve it. I really blew this year. I wish I had a teacher again."

"Yitz," said Rabbi Rosenthal kindly, "If the only thing you learned this year was that human beings deserve respect, it was worth the entire show."

"Show?" Yitz gulped.

"You're a smart boy, Yitz. Did you really think Yeshiva Darchei Avos would accept all of our eighth grade students, one by one? We ran our class out of their building for the last two months. They're still our students. It was the only way we could prove to each boy how important it is to have a *rebbi*. Now all of your classmates will be happy to return to our school and you can graduate with your class."

And at last, Yitz was ready to admit it. Rabbi Rosenthal was smarter than he.

Mazal Tov?

"NOW TURN AROUND AND LOOK IN THIS MIRROR," Gigi instructed Fraidy. "Good?"

Simi watched as Fraidy spun around, the hem of the white organza gown just hovering over the floor, her older sister's chestnut brown hair cascading over the white collar, her face aglow. "I can't believe it's me!" bubbled Fraidy.

"They all say that. They're all the same," Gigi chuckled to Mommy, her gold tooth flashing. The rich, the poor, even the difficult-to-fit girls knew that Gigi could make the most nervous *kalla* comfortable in her boutique. Years of servicing brides and their families gave her experience at putting any customer at ease. "My, but she will be a beautiful *kalla*. Your first?"

"First girl after four boys," said Mommy. "Our oldest daughter. And here," she added, putting her hand on Simi's shoulder, is our youngest daughter. She's here for a gown as well."

"Young ladies' gowns are hanging in the other room. She looks like she's in ninth grade? Growing your hair for the wedding?" Simi nodded at Gigi's guesses. Ever since the engagement, she had refused to submit to a haircut so her hair would be long enough for the up-do hairstyle she dreamed of. "You can go look by yourself and take your time deciding what you want while we work with this blushing bride. I'll come in a few minutes to help."

While Mommy and Gigi turned their attention to Fraidy, Simi went into the second room of Gigi's Gowns. She gently felt each hanging gown – the off-white masterpiece loaded with sequins, the elegant black evening dress, the shiny grey two-piece floor length jumper -- and then her eye fell on a gorgeous bright blue gown, with a high neck and flowing sleeves. It would match her blue eyes perfectly. She could just picture herself in the gown, with little blue clips scattered about her long hair, curled upward in twirls and then cascading down in fancy curls. "I found it!" she called happily.

"What? So fast?" asked Gigi. "Bring it here then, and your mother will help you try it on."

Carefully, Simi took the gown from the rack and went to the dressing room. It looked like something out of a fairy tale – and, with a few small alterations, it would fit like a dream!

"Are you sure, Simi? You look wonderful, but wouldn't you like to try on another one – just to compare?" asked her mother.

"I'm sure," said Simi. "I love it! Oh, I can't wait until the *chasuna*!" She spun around in her gown and then rushed over and hugged her sister. "I am so excited!"

Fraidy smiled. "So am I, Simi."

"You're all set, then," said Gigi, "Take the veil with you and I'll come around to your house a week before the wedding with the gowns to do the final alterations. Good?"

"Great," said Mommy. "Thank you very much! And now," she said, looking at a long list she pulled from her pocketbook, "onward to the housewares store for garbage cans."

"Mommy," said Simi with a slight cough, "uh…as much as I'd really love to shop for garbage cans, do you think you can drop me off by Rochel's house to study? We have a social studies test tomorrow."

"Rochel's house? You mean your home-away-from-home? No problem, Simi," said Mommy. "Her house is on the way to the store. Do you want to call first?"

"Nah. Rochel's always happy to see me."

Mommy and Fraidy laughed. It was true. Rochel and Simi practically lived in each others' houses ever since their families were neighbors in the newlywed apartment complex. Since the families moved to single family homes, next door to each other, the two girls acted like sisters. They practically mixed up whose last name was whose as they advanced through grade school and camp, doing everything together from studying to skipping rope.

The car pulled up outside Rochel's house, and Mommy waited to see Simi's nod by the door indicating that it was a good time for Rochel to study. Then she drove off, happy for Simi that she would be spared the excruciating decisions ahead for that day, like which color handle the *milchig* spatula should have, and how many rolls of contact paper would be needed to cover the inside of six drawers.

"Hi, Simi," Rochel greeted her. "I brought the social studies book home. Come on into the kitchen where we can study in peace."

"Great," said Simi. "And I'm glad you don't mind my not calling first. I've had it with shopping! My sister seems to think all the stores are going out of business the day after her *sheva brochos* are over. She's going to own so much stuff, I can't imagine where it's all going to fit. But," she remembered, her eyes lighting up, "wait 'til I tell you about the gown fitting this morning! I chose the first one I tried on!" She proceeded to regal Rochel with every single detail about the fabric and cut, even drawing a picture on a napkin from the kitchen holder.

"Simi. Social studies, remember? We don't have all day," Rochel finally interrupted impatiently.

Simi looked up in surprise. "I thought you were into gowns," she said, a bit hurt. "I remember you getting excited about *your* gown when your sister got married last year."

Rochel shrugged. "Whatever. Come on. Here's a map of the

world. We're supposed to memorize all the countries in the Americas, know their capitol cities, and recognize their borders. North America is easiest. United States – Washington, D.C., Canada ..."

The girls threw themselves into their work, reciting countries and tracing maps, and then stopped for an energy break. "Ma?" called Rochel. "Can we take cake from the freezer?"

"No. It's for Shabbos," came the answer.

"Who's that?" Simi asked. "That didn't sound like your mother."

"Whatever," said Rochel. "Let's eat some *nosh* instead." She pulled a chair over to the *nosh* cabinet, climbed up, and started rummaging around.

"Okay, I'm not starving. But really, Rochel-- Who was that?"

"My sister," Rochel said. "You want pretzel rods or potato chips?"

"Pretzels. How long is your sister here visiting?"

Rochel climbed down from the chair. She stood with the pretzel bag in her hand. "She's not visiting. Okay? How many do you want?"

"Three, thanks, but what do you mean she's not visiting? I just heard her voice."

Rochel took a few pretzels out of the bag, put them on the table, climbed back up on the chair, replaced the bag, climbed back down, and opened the refrigerator. "Orange juice or soda?"

"Orange juice," said Simi. "You know I never drink soda."

"Oh, right."

The girls crunched their snack in silence.

"So, how long is she here for?" asked Simi again.

"Who?" asked Rochel.

"Your sister."

"Do you want to do Central America next or South America?"

"Rochel. What's going on?" asked Simi, a sudden fear gripping her heart.

Rochel looked down. "I don't want to talk about it."

"Is she okay?"

"What does 'okay' mean? She got divorced. So she came back home. I don't know anything else about it. Nobody tells me anything, okay? So what else do *you* want to know?" Rochel stared threateningly at Simi, her arms crossed over her chest.

"Uh… what else? Uh… uh…" Simi fumbled with her pretzels. "Uh…I wonder what's the capitol city of Mexico?"

"This is the perfect salad recipe for *sheva brochos*," Mommy said one night after dinner, flipping through her recipe book. "What do you think, Simi? You're the one who's going to make it. Do you think we should add in nuts or craisins?"

"What *sheva brochos*?" Simi mumbled.

"Why… why the *sheva brochos* we're making for Fraidy and Zev!" answered her mother, looking up in surprise. "Did you forget that your sister is getting married in two weeks?"

"Uh, yeah. I guess I forgot," said Simi. "I'm going upstairs to get my briefcase and then can I run over to Rochel's house to do my homework?"

"Fine, Simi. I'll go upstairs with you," she said, closing the recipe book. "I told Fraidy I'd help her clean out her room. The big day is coming soon."

"Big day? What big day?" muttered Simi as she followed her mother up the steps.

Fraidy was already in her room, wearing an old model's coat, crocks, and her veil – for practice – on her head. She was standing in the middle of a pile of albums, papers, cassettes, sweaters, notebooks, and shoes for all seasons, flipping the pages of an old scrapbook.

"Mommy, do you think I should bring my all my scrapbooks with me? Do you think Zev will enjoy seeing pictures of me in camp when I was twelve years old?" she asked, fingering the page with a smile. "But I look so *nebby* here. The styles were so silly back then. I don't know if I want him to see me wearing a purple skirt instead of a black one."

Simi stopped by the bedroom door for a moment and heard Mommy respond as she looked up from the drawer she was emptying. "Up to you, Fraidy. You can leave whatever you don't want to take to your new apartment in our basement. It'll wait here until you claim it."

"It's such a big job to pack up twenty-two years worth of stuff," Fraidy said, plunking down on her bed. "I'm going to miss this room. Wow. I can still remember when we tried to put on the wallpaper and it got so miserably stuck to itself that we ended up painting. And I remember the mouse that lived under my dresser; and how we had that eighth grade sleep over party and three kids threw up so we got rid of the carpet."

Mommy groaned. "I hope you have some happy memories of your room to take with you too!"

"Oh, Mommy. Of course! I love this room! The sun wakes me up in the morning, shining through the window. And each day, since we moved into this house from our old apartment, I've peeked out to check the weather. From up here, I could always see the clouds blowing in from the ocean, or the leaves changing, or the first white blossoms of the cherry tree right outside the window. Then the smell of breakfast would reach me from the stairs. I always jumped right out of bed if I smelled pancakes," she reminisced with a smile.

"Yes, you were always the first down on pancake mornings," Mommy chuckled in agreement.

"If you ask me, this is the nicest room in the house. I've done years of homework at this desk," she said, patting the old, worn, wooden piece of furniture, "and I've had so many friends sleep over on the futon in the closet. And Mommy…I can still hear the echoes of years of tuck-ins. I think the words of *Shema* must be embedded in the walls… and the 'I love you's' that were said with it every single night. I'm going to miss these walls!" she said, throwing her hands out as if to embrace them.

"Don't miss them too much," muttered Simi, as she passed by with her briefcase on the way to Rochel's house. "You might see them again soon."

"What's with Simi?" Fraidy asked Mommy.

Mommy shrugged. "She has been acting a little grumpy lately. Maybe she needs more attention. A *kalla* in the house certainly monopolizes a mother's time. Come on… let's tackle the closet. Keep or toss?" she asked, holding up a hooded coat.

★★★

"Naturally the *kalla* has lost weight," smiled Gigi. She had come with the gowns, just as she had promised, a week before the wedding, to make the final alterations. "Just a pin here, and a tuck there…good?" She pulled in the dress at the sides. "I'll have it back to you tomorrow. And now the little one in the electric blue. Let's see you try it on, sweets," said Gigi, holding out the gown Simi had chosen.

Simi moped near the door. "It's fine."

"Come now. Spend a minute trying it on, and we'll make sure it still fits and you haven't grown," Gigi pressed, pin box in hand.

"I don't want to," Simi said.

"Simi," warned Mommy, "I know it takes energy, but Gigi's here, and if you don't try it on now…"

"I don't care about my gown!" Simi suddenly shouted. "I don't care about the wedding! *I don't even want to go to the wedding!*" She burst out sobbing, and ran to her room.

The embarrassed silence was broken by Gigi. "They all say that. They're all the same," she chuckled. "She'll try it on when I come back tomorrow. Good?" She brushed off her skirt, packed up her supplies, took only Fraidy's gown to alter and left. The minute she was out of sight, Mommy ran up to Simi's room, gave a little knock, sat down on the edge of the bed next to her daughter, and handed her a tissue to wipe her eyes.

"I think we have to talk." she began, a look of concern evident in her features, her eyes trained on Simi's face. "What is it, Simi, dear? What happened? You loved that gown! Why aren't you excited about the *simcha*?"

And at last, with a sniff and a sob, the whole story burst out: how she had been at Rochel's sister's wedding, and how gorgeous they all looked, and how she had no clue why but all of a sudden Rochel's sister was back home, and how if people could get married and then divorced, then all the food and fuss and fanciness weren't worth anything at all.

"I don't know," she concluded with a sigh, "why everybody calls a wedding 'a *simcha*'! I think a wedding is just one big question mark!" She stopped, and then looked to her mother with pleading eyes. "What happened to Rochel's sister, Mommy? What went wrong?" Her voice rose, begging to understand, desperate for comfort.

Her mother's face registered surprise, and then comprehension. "I certainly hope that Rochel's sister will remarry soon," she said, "but you and I will never really know what happened. It's not really our business, is it?" she added gently, but firmly, "so there's nothing to talk about. Outsiders never really know the truth," she repeated as she shook her head. "I'm sorry, dear. I know it's painful."

"Well then, can't you at least promise me that Fraidy will never get divorced?"

Mommy paused, and then said softly, "There *are* no guarantees in life, Simi. I can't promise."

"But then why go through all this wedding stuff?" asked Simi with a moan. "Maybe we should save the celebration for their fiftieth wedding anniversary. Then it'll be safe to be happy."

Mommy laughed. "Can you imagine Fraidy as a seventy-two year old *kalla* in a white gown? My darling Simi, marriage is based on hope -- but not hope alone. We've tried to prepare Fraidy since the moment she was born by trying to set in an example in our family about how to be respectful, patient, and forgiving. She's learned and absorbed Torah values about life and marriage, and she knows what it means to be a giver. It's time for her to move on in life. Marriage is a wonderful opportunity."

Simi nodded slowly.

"She and Zev have a lot in common and want the same things out of life," Mommy continued. "He certainly seems to be her *bashert*..."

Mommy's voice trailed off as she looked far into the distance. Simi waited... and waited... She began to wonder if her mother had forgotten she was sitting there, or had fallen asleep with her eyes open, when her mother suddenly smiled and gave her a big hug. "And we have to *daven*. With *Hashem*'s help, we think that Fraidy and Zev will make a wonderful couple and build a beautiful, new Jewish home. What bigger *simcha* could there be? It's okay to be happy, Simi."

"Well, in that case," said Simi, with a sigh of relief, a toss of her ponytail, "I'll try on the gown again. And, Mommy?"

"Yes, sweetheart."

"If Fraidy *really* is moving out for good...can I have her room?"

Bye, Ma! Have a Great Shabbos!

"SHAINDY, PLEASE PUT AWAY YOUR SHOES," said Mommy as she passed through the dining room with her arms full of laundry.

Shaindy was holding a paintbrush, wet with red paint, in mid-air above the letters '*Moshiach* Week.' "Soon, Ma. I just have to finish this poster." She carefully filled in the outlined words and sat back.

Being a counselor in Camp Schmamp was just about the best thing that ever happened to her, Shaindy thought blissfully. She was spending her summer with most of her best friends from school, but without the pressure of tests to study for and homework to do. And this was an important summer, they all knew. By next year, after twelfth grade, they'd all be dispersing; some of them would be packing to go far away for seminary, some of them would already enter the work force, and, she thought with a jolt, some of them might even be "senior-*kallahs*," getting engaged during twelfth grade and getting married next summer! To be spending this summer running relay races, screaming cheers from on top of benches and chairs, and giving over the '*mesorah*' of the different levels of Chinese jump rope to the next generation of campers was the ultimate in fun.

Not only that, but she was making money. Camp Schmamp paid their counselors well, and, if she included the tips that hopefully would come in, she would be able to spend some of the money on a trip with her friends the last week of summer vacation, and still have enough to put away to make her parents happy.

"Shaindy," her mother interrupted her thoughts as she returned to the dining room, accompanied by her little brother Aharon Boruch, (nicknamed AB by his older brother Peretz when the latter was learning the ABC's.) "Didn't I ask you to move your shoes? They're right in the middle of the floor where anyone could trip on them."

Shaindy sighed. "And I'm right in the middle of painting. Can't AB pick them up?"

"They're your shoes, Shaindy," Mommy said with a frown. "I'm taking AB to his swimming lesson now. Please answer the phone and write down messages, okay?" And she was off.

Shaindy dramatically put her paintbrush into the water, slowly lumbered over to her shoes, picked them up and plunked them on the bottom step.

Yes, putting away some of the money she made this summer would make her parents happy, but making them happy was getting more and more difficult. It wasn't that they were mean or unreasonable, Shaindy knew, but it was things like being told to put away her shoes – now – that made her feel that her parents really didn't understand her. She was a year away from graduation, already working, responsible for twenty squawking second graders from ten o'clock in the morning to three in the afternoon every day. She didn't want to be told not to eat dessert before the meal or where to put her shoes!

My goodness, she grumbled to herself as she finished her poster, she was already grown up. She already knew how to drive, even though her parents wouldn't allow her to get her license, and in a little more than a year, she'd be able to vote in elections like all full-blown adults. And here she was being treated the same way as her kid brothers and sisters! When would her mother realize how grown-up she was and give her more independence?

After camp the next day, Shaindy sighed as she dutifully called her mother to tell her that she was going over to Rifky's house to work out the *Moshiach* activities for the next day in camp.

"Fine," her mother said, "but please be home in time for dinner at six o'clock so we can all eat together. Tatty and I have something we have to discuss with the family."

As Shaindy and Rifky cut out little bricks to build a *Bais Hamikdash*, folded white donkeys, and wrapped the little chocolate shofars that would be scattered all over the bunk room for the children to find, Shaindy shared her resentment. "Imagine. Not only do I have to call to ask my mother if I can come to work here after camp, but she tells me: 'Be home in time for dinner.' I'm practically seventeen! If I don't come home in time, I'll make myself scrambled eggs or have a bowl of cereal. After all, during the nine days, it's only going to be *milchigs*. No barbeque or anything."

Rifky looked down as she snipped an aqua brick. "Seems to me like your mother is just being nice, but I wouldn't know. In my house, with ten kids, we never eat together."

The girls snipped and chatted until 5:55, and then Shaindy ran home, arriving out of breath at 6:07. "On time enough?" she asked out of breath as she ran into the kitchen. and skidded to a stop. Her father, already at his place at the head of the table, looked up with disapproval. Her mother was standing, holding a huge bowl of spaghetti. Her sisters, Perel and Ruchy were already eating – Perel, her favorite vegetables out of the salad, and Ruchy was already up to dessert. AB and Peretz were fighting over the ketchup.

"On time enough," sighed her mother. "Wash up quick. Tatty has a *chavrusa* in a half an hour and we need time to talk."

Shaindy washed her hands, sat down, and filled her bowl with lettuce and tomatoes and wondered what possibly could be the topic of this discussion. No one looked too sad or too nervous –

which was a good sign. No one looked worried. If anyone were in trouble, her parents would never handle it publicly. Shaindy took some spaghetti and convinced AB to share the ketchup before her father began.

"This is the question," said Tatty, before her imagination could wander too far. "We've been invited to a *bar mitzva* for *Shabbos Nachamu*."

"*Mazal tov*," said Shaindy dutifully.

"What should I wear?" Perel whined. At almost fifteen, it was important to plan this two weeks in advance.

"Can we wear matching?" Ruchy begged. At eight, her grandest wish was to be like her sister.

"*Parshas Vo'eschanan*," said Peretz. "That's a long one." At thirteen, he was quite aware of which *parshios* carried the biggest burdens for his classmates.

"Whose *bar mitzva*?" asked AB. "And can I come… please?" At five, the baby of the family, he was keenly aware of the possibility of not having been included in the invitation.

"Well," said Tatty, "you see, um… It's cousin Zanvil's *bar mitzva*…It's going to be in a hotel."

Peretz's eyes lit up. "I've never been in a hotel for *Shabbos*. You think there's horse back riding on Sunday?"

"Whoa!" said Perel. "This is going to be one fancy event. I think I'll need a new outfit! And I can't go shopping before *Tisha B'av!*"

"I don't you need to go shopping," Mommy faltered. "You see …"

"The fact is," Tatty continued, "that only Mommy and I were invited. No kids."

Five faces around the table fell. "Oh."

"We've never left you kids for *Shabbos* before," said Tatty, "but Zanvil is my only brother's only son. I don't really have a choice whether to go or not."

"So the question really is whether I should go with Tatty,"

said Mommy, "or if I should stay home with you kids."

"Home!" begged AB.

"Home!" said Ruchy.

"I could go instead of Mommy," Peretz offered hopefully.

Perel sighed and went back to her spaghetti. There was no new outfit involved so it really didn't matter.

Only Shaindy smiled. "Of course you should go, Mommy!" she said. "What's the big deal? I'm going into twelfth grade. I'll manage with the kids just fine."

Mommy looked at her with a mix of gratitude and doubt. "Really? I would love to go away with Tatty. I mean, of course, I would miss you all VERY much, but..."

"We'll be fine!" Shaindy said brightly. "Right kids?" She looked around the table, with a smile that barred no refusal. "You deserve a break, Ma. You should go and have a great time."

Tatty and Mommy looked at each other with a look of relief. "You really don't mind?" Tatty asked. "It's a lot of responsibility."

"Responsible is my middle name," Shaindy replied. "It will be my pleasure."

The next two weeks flew by. The nine days came and went with their sorrow and sadness, and then *erev Shabbos* the washing machine worked non-stop, doing its part to refresh the household and the world. Along with the cleaning, Mommy was hurriedly packing for their *Shabbos* away from home.

"Peretz," she called, "can you bring me the blue suitcase with the garment holder inside, please?"

Peretz lugged the old bag up from the basement, and Mommy began loading in what she and Tatty would need for Shabbos. The kids all gravitated to the dining room table to watch the unfamiliar occurrence.

"You're bringing that?" asked Perel.

"What's wrong?" asked Mommy, surprised.

"Ma, no one wears purple suits anymore. Everyone wears black."

"But… but it's my favorite suit."

"It's ancient!" Perel insisted.

"It fits," said Mommy, and she clipped it into the buckle and closed the suitcase.

Tatty came into the house, swinging his keys. "Ready, Mommy? We've got to get going if we don't want to hit too much traffic."

Mommy looked around at her gang. "Good bye, AB," she said with a hug and a kiss. "Make sure to listen to Shaindy. Bye, Ruchy. Be good and don't eat too much junk food. Be good, Peretz. Mr. and Mrs. Niman said they'll come for the *seuda* on Shabbos, so don't leave *shul* without them, okay? I think it will be nice for you to have some adults here for one meal." Shaindy wrinkled her nose, but her mother continued her last instructions. "Perel, see if you can finish these four loads of laundry before Shabbos…And Shaindy. How can I thank you? Don't forget that Mrs. Goldstein is next door if you need anything, Oh, kids, I'm going to miss you!"

"The car is all packed up, Mommy," Tatty announced. "Uh, Mommy? You're not going to cry, are you? It's only one Shabbos. We'll be back early Sunday morning."

"No, no tears," she said, wiping away something suspicious from her cheek. "Any problems, call us on the cell phone. I love you all! Have a great Shabbos!"

"You too, Mommy," they chorused, with Shaindy the loudest of all.

The kids stood waving to the car until it turned the corner, and then, with a sort of empty feeling, turned to go back into the house. All but Shaindy. She turned cripslyl, marched the kids in before her, and made sure the door was locked. She was finally in charge, finally the adult at home. Since that memorable family dinner discussion, she had been dreaming of this moment of independence.

"Perel, you heard Mommy. Please keep feeding the washing machine. And Peretz, move your shoes," she said, pointing to his misplaced footwear. "We have four hours until Shabbos. I'm going to make the chicken and the *cholent* now. Ruchy," Shaindy continued in her take-charge tone, "I'm going to give you a special Shabbos job. Go to the grocery down the block and pick out your favorite something for dessert. You can take your friend from next door with you."

"Don't I need money?" Ruchy asked.

"I don't have any cash on me. Just tell Mr. Bloom to write it down on our account and Mommy will pay when she gets home on Sunday."

"Okay," said Ruchy. "I hope I'll be able to carry everything home," she added, but Shaindy was already rushing to make the beds and peel the potatoes for her special *cholent* when she noticed her little brother sitting in the kitchen corner. "Hey! AB! What's the matter? Why are you crying?"

"I miss Mommy!" he wailed.

"Already?" she asked in surprise. "Here. Have a candy." She reached up high in the *nosh* cabinet and handed him a treat he normally only saw on Shabbos afternoon. "Let's get to work."

That *erev* Shabbos, the five children rose to the occasion, helping so much that their mother would have been surprised. Shaindy thoroughly enjoyed being in charge, and Peretz, Perel, Ruchy and AB were amazingly cooperative. Finally, the moment came for Shaindy to *bentch licht* in her mother's place. Peretz took AB to *shul*, and the girls finished setting the table.

It was strange, alright, to be on their own. However when the boys came home, Peretz made *kiddush*, sounding exactly like his father, if you didn't count the cracking voice, and Shaindy served one course after the next, just like her mother, and Peretz even read the *parsha* sheets the kids had brought home from camp. *Shabbos* almost felt normal.

"Mommy and Tatty could go away more often," Shaindy said as she cleared away the *bentchers* after the meal. "I think we can manage fine without them."

"Good for you. I'm going out to learn," said Peretz.

"But you didn't help clean up. And, that means I'll have to wait up for you to come home," Shaindy complained. "Can't you just learn at home?"

"Nope. But don't wait up for me," said Peretz, and he slammed the door on his way out.

Shaindy sighed. "Teenagers," she muttered, and then bit her tongue. She sounded just like her mother. "Okay. Perel, you clean up the table while I get Ruchy and AB to bed."

"I don't want to go to sleep now," said Ruchy.

"Me neither," said AB.

"Want to hear a story and then go to sleep?" Shaindy asked with a convincing smile.

The two children sat beside her and listened to one story, and then insisted on a second and a third. "Mommy always reads this one," AB insisted. "If we say please, she always reads one more," Ruchy said, "so ple-e-e-ease….?"

Shaindy pushed forward through a fourth story and a fifth. "Bed time now" she practically begged.

But the kids knew when they had the advantage. "One more! One more!" they chorused. As Shaindy's voice became softer and softer, Ruchy leaned her head on Shaindy's right shoulder and AB slid down and put his head on her lap. At last, after forty five minutes of reading, they were finally…

"One more!" AB started up again in his dreams.

As gently as she could, Shaindy moved AB to his bed, and motioned to Perel to help Ruchy sleepwalk toward hers. "I'm going to let them just sleep in their clothes," Shaindy said as she walked back into the dining room. "Wow, am I tired. I don't know how Mommy does this every single night. Hey, Perel. You didn't finish clearing the dishes."

"Sorry, Shaindy. I used all my energy up doing laundry this afternoon. Plus, I must find out what happened in the latest *frum* novel. The Israeli spies are just about to discover the secret that the Russian scientists have been working on deep in a cave on the north pole."

"What's so *frum* about that novel?" Shaindy asked as she picked up the now-dried pickles and bits of challa from the table.

"They *daven mincha* before they go out on their missions," Perel replied as she curled up in Shaindy's favorite corner of the couch and got lost in the pages of her book.

"I wonder where Peretz is," Shaindy said aloud. "It's already midnight. Perel what do you think?" But Perel had fallen asleep – in her clothes – with the book open on her lap. "I wonder at what point I should begin to worry... Should I go bother Mrs. Goldstein? That would be silly. He just went out to learn and, after all, it is *Shabbos Nachamu*. Maybe he met a friend. But it's midnight already and he's only thirteen... On the other hand, he told me not to worry, so I suppose he meant it. On the other hand..."

Shaindy looked out the window. Her brother was nowhere in sight. "Should I stay up and wait for him? Or should I go to sleep... but then do I leave the door unlocked?" She nibbled a piece of cake and fought with herself. In the end, she lay down on the couch, and just before she fell asleep, she wondered why her parents ever bothered to buy pajamas and nightgowns for their family.

Sometime during the night she woke up, discovered Peretz was in bed, and locked all the doors. In the morning, she quizzed him on his late night adventures.

"I was learning, Shaindy. Then I went to a *shalom zachor* for the Brizel's new baby boy, and then came home. Boy! You sound just like Mommy! Come on, AB, let's get going. Time for *shul*."

For a second, Shaindy was too speechless to reply. "Just remember to bring Rabbi and Mrs. Niman home with you from *shul*," she sputtered after him as he left.

"I know, I know, Just like Mommy," he whispered to AB, and they giggled together on their way out the door.

Shaindy *davened*, and then woke up Ruchy and Perel. "Come help set the table, kids."

Perel turned over. "Shabbos morning I sleep late," she said with finality.

"Aren't you going to help, Ruchy? Remember all those books I read you last night? Can't you at least help a bit?"

The only response was a sleepy murmur, so Shaindy managed to get the table set before the company came, without any help.

"It looks delicious," said Mrs. Niman. "My husband practically lives for his *Shabbos cholent*."

"I made it myself," said Shaindy, and then she added her mother's line. "You know what they say: The *cholent* is as good as the guests." She watched as the large steaming serving bowl was passed around the table and everyone took a good size portion. There was just enough left when it was her turn to take. Mmmmm. She slid a potato and piece of meat onto her plate and looked around the table proudly.

Why wasn't anyone eating? Why were they all suddenly filling their drinking glasses with whatever drink was closest to their place?

She took a tiny taste of the food on her plate. Yuch! What a strange taste! And then suddenly, ouch! She also reached desperately for a drink, while at the same time, apologizing to the guests. "Oh, I'm sorry, Rabbi and Mrs. Niman. I don't know what happened. Perel, quickly help me clear off the plates. I think we have some cold cuts to serve instead. Oh, I'm sorry!" Tears filled her eyes as she rushed into the kitchen.

"It's horrible!" she moaned to Perel. "What happened to my *cholent*, Perel?" She looked at her sister, who was trying to look in any direction, and finally settled on an invisible spot just above Shaindy's head. "Perel! Do you know something I don't know?"

"Well, uh… it's just that Peretz said he wanted the cholent to taste like Chap-A-Bite's *cholent* and I think he was experimenting a little while you were giving AB his bath yesterday afternoon. He thought that hot pepper juice would give it a spicy taste. That and a few tablespoons of horse radish. And the extra bottle of beer left over in the pantry. Oh, don't worry, Shaindy. No one will be hungry once we serve dessert."

Perel was right, of course. No one could be hungry after being served Ruchy's favorites: three different brands of *kokosh* cake, and three different flavors of *parve* ice cream. "You said buy my favorite, and I couldn't remember which it was," she explained to Shaindy. "But now I remember. It was the green one." And she scooped spoon after spoon of apple crisp flavored ice cream onto her plate.

By the time Shabbos was over, Shaindy had spent hours refereeing, serving snacks, cleaning up, and even bandaging AB's gushing forehead. After *havdala,* she reached for the phone and called her mother, hoping for just a word of reassurance.

"No service available," the automated voice said again and again.

Shaindy took a deep breath, and began the bed-time-clean-up procedure for the second night in a row, humming to herself the *Moshiach* song she had taught her campers that week. "And even though he may tarry, I wait for him each day," only by 'him' she meant her parents, and boy, did she hope they'd come soon. By two in the morning, the house was pulled together and she fell into an exhausted sleep.

When Mommy and Tatty arrived home Sunday morning, there was a big 'Welcome Home' sign taped to the front door. As the car pulled into the driveway, Peretz, Perel, and Ruchy ran down the steps to greet their parents, followed by AB, still in his pajamas.

"It's so good to be home!" said Mommy, hugging everyone at once. "I missed you all so much. And no, Perel, I was not the only one in a purple suit." She looked around at her brood with a huge grin, and then suddenly noticed an absence. "Hey. Where's Shaindy?"

AB pointed to the doorway, where Shaindy was standing, leaning on the door frame with a tired look on her face.

"Shaindy! How was it?" asked Mommy. "I'm sorry our cell phone didn't work in the mountains. Did you manage without us?"

Shaindy smiled. She had mentally rehearsed her line so many times it flowed smoothly from her lips. "We were fine, *boruch Hashem*. I'm glad you had a good time."

And I'm glad you're back, she thought silently to herself. I sure won't mind being a kid again —for just a little longer. It's pretty nice to have a mother around after all.

A Spoiled Summer

UT I WANT TO GO TO CAMP!" Bentzion shouted. His face was bright red as he jumped up and knocked the kitchen chair against the wall.

Bentzion's father and mother shifted in their seats. "Bentzion," said his father as he pursed his lips. "That's no way for a *ben Torah* to respond to his parents."

"I don't CARE!" Bentzion shouted.

Bentzion caught his mother's eye. She looked so sad, so sorry. "It's not FAIR!" he continued to wail. It wasn't fair of him either, he knew, to pressure his parents like this, especially since they had just explained so clearly that there was absolutely no money available this summer and that he would get his turn soon enough – maybe even next summer. But he didn't care. "Every kid in this family waits until their *bar mitzva* or *bas mitzva*, and then they get to go to camp. Shimmy went when he was thirteen, and so did Avi. Shayna and Minky both went the summer they turned twelve. Now all of a sudden when it's finally my turn, the rules CHANGE!"

"The economy changed…" his mother began.

"I don't CARE about the economy!" Bentzion stormed.

"Look, Benzy," she tried again. "If you really want to go so much, I can see if I can get you a job part-time in camp, like an assistant for the younger bunks, and then it should cost less...."

"I don't WANT to work!" Bentzion said. "Everyone else went to camp and had a blast. Why should I have to work?! Is it my fault I was born last and all the money got used up before I got to go to camp?"

"Bentzion," he father commanded, with a very stern voice, "that's enough. Go to your room."

Bentzion banged the chair into the wall once more, and, leaving his dirty dinner plate on the table, he stormed out of the kitchen. "'Go to your room! Go to your room!'" he practically cried on his way up the stairs. "I don't *want* to go to my room! I want to go to CAMP!"

"It's not like him," he heard his mother say. "Maybe we should have been gentler?"

"Gentler than what?" his father grimaced. "No camp means no camp. That kid is spoiled rotten."

The next thing his parents heard was the bedroom door slamming, and the sound of Bentzion throwing himself onto his bed. He pulled the pillow over his head to block out the rest of the conversation. He wasn't spoiled! His *summer* was spoiled! Sure, camp was expensive and this was not the year for extra expenses. But he was wickedly disappointed! And he wanted everyone to know it.

Later at night, Avi came into the room and flicked on the light. "How come you're sleeping in your clothes, Bentzion?" he asked. "And did you *daven maariv*?" Bentzion rolled over slowly. "What time is it?"

"Ten o'clock. You feeling okay?"

"Just about as okay as a prisoner condemned to hang."

"Sounds bad. What happened? You failed your eighth grade graduation practice?"

"Worse. No camp this summer."

Avi sighed in sympathy. "Sorry to hear."

"Easy for you to say," Bentzion groaned. "You know I've been looking forward to camp for thirteen years, and now the opportunity has been grabbed from my fingers by an evil economy."

"You've been looking forward to camp since you were born? I think you may be exaggerating, Benz. Why don't you just think of something else to do for the summer? How about getting a job like me?"

"No one will hire me. Even you had a hard time finding that job in Frum Foods, and you're eighteen-- *and* you've worked summers for other caterers. You know they're saying this year that all the jobs that traditionally go to teenagers are going to people in their twenties who are desperate for work, and all the jobs that used to be taken by college grads are now being grabbed up by grown-ups with families. Plus," Bentzion said with a flourish, "the only thing I have experience in is making mischief in school. How does that translate into a job?"

"You're not such a mischief maker," Avi said. "As a matter of fact, the rumors I hear are that my little brother is the serious learning type, never wasting a minute. Why don't you spend your summer vacation in the *beis medrash*?"

Bentzion thought for a moment. It was true he loved to learn, but he was angry. Every American Jewish kid went to overnight camp, didn't they? Why should he be deprived? "Nope. I think I'm going to spend the summer in bed. I'll sleep late in the morning, eat breakfast, take a mid-morning nap. And then after eating lunch, maybe I'll play on the computer and then take another nap. And then I'll go out for a late *maariv* so I don't wake up too early in the morning." He stretched and pulled the covers over his head.

Avi threw a pillow at Bentzion. "Mommy and Tatty are going to love your plans," he said. "I think first you'd better go *daven maariv*. And then you'll probably do what everyone else does who can't get a job."

"What's that?" asked Bentzion, peeking out from under the blanket.

"Start your own business," Avi laughed.

Bentzion threw the pillow back, pulled himself out of bed, went downstairs, and poked his head into the kitchen. "Bye, Ma. I'm going to find out where there's a 10:30 *minyan* for *maariv*."

"Are you okay, Bentzion?" his mother asked worriedly. "I'm sorry to see you so upset. You weren't quite yourself there."

"Yeah, I'm fine, Ma," he replied, and then, remembering that his *father* was the one who thought he was spoiled, he slid his dirty plate into the sink and added, "I'm sorry, too."

"It's okay. *Daven* well…"

"Bye."

The air was pleasant and cool outside. It was good to get out and see something besides his own four walls. The streets weren't empty yet, and there was the regular foot traffic of men coming and going to various *maariv minyanim* in the city. Bentzion was happy that he lived in the city where there was some action, where if you missed one *minyan* you could always catch the next, where there was more than grass and trees to commune with on the street.

He walked down his own block, past one *shteible* and the next. *Anshei Milchama* was closed, and the sign on the door of *Bnei Mukdam* indicated that their last *maariv minyan* had been at 9:00. Bentzion turned the corner onto the avenue and continued his search.

A few blocks down, he saw a bunch of boys who were a few years older than he, who used to be in his elementary school. He recognized Moishie and Ephraim in the middle of the group. They had certainly grown taller, and they were standing on the street corner, not looking like they were in any particular rush.

"Uh… hi, Moishe. You know of a *minyan* for *maariv* around here?"

"It's Mo, kid. Do I know you?"

"Uh, yeah," said Bentzion, beginning to feel kind of uncomfortable. "You used to be in my yeshiva. You and Ephraim were a year behind my brother Avi, I think."

"Ephraim? You mean Pogo here? Yeah, we've been out of school for a while."

Suddenly Bentzion noticed that Mo and Pogo both had cigarettes in their hands, and no *yarmulkas* on their heads! He gave a quick half smile and started to walk away.

"Hey, kid. I thought you wanted to know about *maariv*," Mo called. "Hold on a minute. Want to try a smoke?"

"Uh… no thanks… I mean, uh… I think I see a *shul* open over there," Bentzion managed to point out, and he began to trot in that direction.

"Well, pray for us too," Pogo called after him.

"I will!" Bentzion shouted back.

Boy, will I ever! he kept thinking as he jogged to the next corner and into the familiar confines of a *beis medrash*. He took a *siddur* from the shelf just in time to join the late *minyan* for *borchu*, and through the entire *maariv* he had no problem including Moishe and Ephraim in his prayers.

In fact, he couldn't forget them or their bare heads. But more importantly, he realized that a long summer of 10:30 PM *maarivs* would give him way too many opportunities to run into them again. For a moment, he considered that smoking would be a great way to get back at his parents for depriving him of camp, but then he regretted entertaining the thought. Even if he were upset with his parents, he didn't want to ruin his own life. Plus, to tell the truth, once the shock of having to stay home for the summer faded, he was able to accept that it wasn't really their fault if they couldn't afford it. His mother really looked sad, and he was pretty sure his father felt bad, too. By the time he walked in the door to his house, Bentzion realized he had better get past the disappointment, pull himself together, and find something to do in the hot months ahead.

★★★

"What should I eat?" he asked his mother again, as he stood

in front of the refrigerator, the door hanging open in his hand, the cool air flowing gently onto his face and chest.

"You mean what should you do?" she asked as she gently closed the door.

"Yeah, I guess so," Bentzion said. "Did you get an answer from Rabbi Gross?"

"He said he has enough counselors for the first half, and he'll see about the second half. Did you talk with Yaakov today? Or Eli? Tatty and I have been very proud of you that you've kept up your morning learning with them in the two weeks since yeshiva was over."

Bentzion sighed. "They left for camp today."

"Oh, right." They both fell silent. "I had another idea, Benz," his mother said. "You're not going to love it, but it might be better than this." 'This' they both knew meant wandering around the house all day, inspecting the contents of the refrigerator once an hour, and groaning a lot.

"Shoot," Bentzion said.

"Rabbi Klein, an old friend of Tatty's, is the rabbi of a *shul* about six blocks away from our house. He also has a ten-year-old son who's sweet as can be," she began.

"But?"

"But he's a little weak in learning. Tatty was talking with him yesterday, and Rabbi Klein said he'd be willing to pay someone to learn with his son, and be a sort of big brother to him. You know, learn for an hour a day, take him out for pizza once a week, maybe practice playing baseball here and there…"

"You don't practice playing baseball, Ma. You just play. Who's paying for the pizza?"

"Rabbi Klein, of course. He realizes that it's not a full day job, so he also would want to hire you to bind some books. He'll show you how," she hurried on. "Between the two jobs, you'll be busy most of the afternoon. Plus, after you finish his books, he'll let you use his drill and tape to bind other people's books. I know it's not camp, but I think it might be a nice opportunity for you," she ended hopefully.

Bentzion sighed. His dreams of a summer in the sun were long gone. Something to do was better than nothing. "Can I charge for the bookbinding, too?" he asked.

"Definitely," his mother said. "Do you want me to call Rabbi Klein?"

"Sure," said Bentzion. "I'll give it a try."

It was worth it to see the smile on his mother's face. One phone call later, Bentzion was hired, and arrangements were made for the boys to meet the next day.

From that afternoon on, Bentzion's day had a blessed schedule. In the morning, he would wake up early to go to *shachris* with his father, come home for breakfast, and then learn on his own for an hour or two. Then he would prepare something to teach to "His Kid."

After lunch, he would walk over to Rabbi Klein's *shul*. There he would meet The Kid and review the *Chumash* and the *mishnayos brochos* that The Kid had learned during the year, and then explore some topics that Bentzion had learned about on his own. Bentzion had never tutored before and, although he was shy in the beginning, so was The Kid, and by the time he got comfortable enough to make a joke, or bring The Klein Kid a can of soda as a treat, the boy was already smiling and begging Bentzion to teach him how to pitch over-handed.

After learning for an hour, Bentzion would go to Rabbi Klein's office. There he would put a CD into the CD player that he had brought, and listen to some good music while he worked on the *seforim*. Sometimes The Kid would stay too, and chatter in the background as Bentzion worked.

The apprenticeship hadn't taken too long. Rabbi Klein showed him how to work the stationary electric drill and make three neat holes in a row, straight through from the front cover, through all the pages, and through the back cover. "See, the holes have to be very close to the spine of the book so that they don't cut into the words, but not too close because then the string won't hold."

Once the holes were drilled, Rabbi Klein showed Bentzion how to thread the strong string through a large needle, and to weave it up through the bottom hole, across the front of the *sefer*, down through the middle hole, across the back, and up through the top hole. Then, the string had to cross the top half of the *sefer*, go back down through the middle hole and up through the bottom. The result was a figure eight, which was tightened just enough to hold the pages without fear of their loosening. Then he neatly knotted the thread and burnt the ends to hold the knot solid.

The next step was to spread the expensive binding tape inside the front and back covers to seal the holes, and then across the spine to make sure that the string would hold safely. He made sure to use the light colored tape on the inside, and the black, shiny tape on the outside.

Last, Bentzion learned how to carefully hold a straight edge razor and cut out the part of the binding tape that covered the title of the *sefer*. "Ah," said Rabbi Klein, as he wound up his demonstration. "You see here: *Bava Metziah*." He gently kissed the *sefer*. "I always bind my new books so they'll last me a long time – maybe even get handed down to my sons." His features saddened for a minute. "I hope."

"He's a great kid," Bentzion said. "I'm sure he'll love to learn *Bava Metziah* some day. We're finishing the *perek Me'aimosai korim* of *Brachos* today. I was thinking of taking him out for Chinese food for a *siyum*," he added.

Rabbi Klein reached into his pocket and pulled out a twenty-dollar bill. "Let me know if it's more than this," he said. "We're so thrilled this arrangement is working out on both sides. Your father assured me you were a nice boy and a good learner. We couldn't be more pleased. And our son really looks forward to your company. Enjoy yourselves, and *mazal tov*."

Bentzion did enjoy himself. He got past the funny feeling of walking on the street with a "little kid" instead of a boy his own age, and they tasted almost everything on the menu. The next day, true to his word, Rabbi Klein filled in the additional twenty-seven dollars. Bentzion was beginning to really enjoy his tutoring position.

Week by week, hour after hour, the summer passed. Often Bentzion found himself taking His Kid for a swim at the JCC, or a bus trip to the park on the other side of town. Rabbi Klein was more than happy to pay for both of them to have a good time, as long as The Kid was enjoying learning and under, what Rabbi Klein called, "the good influence" of a boy as nice as Bentzion. Together they celebrated the *siyum* on *hoyo korai baTorah*, followed by a *siyum* on *mishemaiyso* . For Bentzion, whose parents couldn't afford to be as generous, it was a good way to check out all the different kosher restaurants in town. And it was great, he thought happily, that the *masechta* of *Brachos* had nine chapters.

The bookbinding was interesting too. After finishing all of Rabbi's Klein's *seforim*, he followed his brother Avi's advice, and actually started his own business. All it took was a notice on a few *shul* bulletin boards, and a few phone calls to friends of his father and of Rabbi Klein, that he was available to do bookbinding.

He built up a reputation of doing a neat, clean job for a reasonable price. When the boys came back from the first trip of camp, he had a lot of business, fixing the *gemaras* they had squashed into duffle bags, *shlepped* with them under the trees in dense forests, on the bus trips, and to campfires, although he warned that particular customer "I don't think I can get the smoky smell out."

Sometimes, if the customer was a boy who he knew, he felt the keen disappointment his spoiled summer as if it were a fresh wound, especially if, while the boy was waiting for his *Bava Kama* to be bound, he went on and on about the fishing trips and the late night kitchen raids. Then Bentzion would feel disappointed about what he had missed. But once the boy paid him in full, and went home with a neatly bound *gemara* under his arm, Bentzion felt a nice sense of accomplishment. He had learned a trade. He was making money. Yep. He was feeling pretty good.

★★★

Bentzion stood in Rabbi Klein's office. It was time to say good-bye.

"Well, I guess this is it," Bentzion said to Rabbi Klein and The Kid. "Yeshiva starts again next week and my mother offered to take me shopping for school supplies and a few new pairs of pants. We just finished learning *haro'eh,* the ninth and final *perek* of *brochos*, so it's a good place to stop. It's been a really nice summer," he said with a smile, and he punched The Kid in the arm.

"Why don't you come to our house for dinner tonight, for the last *siyum*?" Rabbi Klein suggested. "We'll make a barbeque. It'll be a nice end-of-the-summer celebration before *rosh chodesh Elul*."

"Please come, Benz," The Kid begged. "Remember how you told me it was a good idea to know *mishnayos* by heart? Well, I memorized the last *mishna* for you."

Bentzion was flattered. What had begun as a business relationship had certainly grown into a real friendship. "Sure! I'd love to come! Let me run home and tell my mother and change my shirt."

An hour later, Bentzion walked up the steps to The Klein Kid's house. He was holding a *sefer Tehilim* that he bought and bound as a gift for His Kid. For a moment, he wondered if he'd ever see him again after the summer. He hoped so. Maybe he'd offer to learn with him on Shabbos afternoons, just to keep up the *kesher* and the relationship.

He rang the bell.

"Come on to the backyard," called a voice. "The barbeque is back here."

The smell of sizzling hamburgers and hotdogs beckoned to Bentzion as he walked down the driveway. There, in the backyard, was a picnic bench, covered with a red and white tablecloth. Red and white balloons were waving merrily from the tree branches. There was a huge amount of potato chips, French fries, watermelon, pickles, ketchup and mustard and *people* there! It took him only a fleeting second to realize that the entire Klein clan was there to celebrate the *siyum*. Good thing he was wearing a clean shirt.

"See, this is Bentzion, Mom," the Klein Kid was saying as he jumped from foot to foot. "See, I told you he was nice," he said as he took the present from Bentzion.

Bentzion smiled pleasantly at Mrs. Klein, and he mumbled, "nice to meet you," but his eyes were fixed on a boy across the yard. "Who's that?" he whispered to The Kid, as soon as they were out of his mother's earshot.

"Oh, that's just my brother Moishie," he answered, "but he likes to be called Mo."

Only then did Bentzion understand how truly important his summer job had been.

★★★

The last day of the summer, Bentzion asked his mother to drive him to the bank to deposit his profits into his *bar mitzva* bank account.

"With money like this," his mother said, "next summer, *im yirtza Hashem*, you'll be able to send yourself to camp. You're still the perfect age. Maybe you'll even be able to go for more than one summer…."

"Thanks, Mommy. We'll see. I might just decide to stay home again," he continued, counting his money. "Nothing wrong with working, you know."

"So you're in business?" his mother asked.

"Yep," he said proudly. "Binding books and big-brother-ing boys."

Which Levine?

BRUCHY AND MALKY NEARLY SKIPPED DOWN THE SIDEWALK in South Rover. "I can't believe it!" said Bruchy for the millionth time as they walked home from Emuna Academy.

"Me neither!" laughed Malky, her brown pony tail dancing in the cold wind.

"And that it's both of us!" added Bruchy, her wide smile gleaming in the sun.

"Together!" ended Malky happily.

The girls rounded the corner to Malky's house. "Let's tell your mother first," said Bruchy. Together the girls burst through the side door. They had been next-door neighbors since they were born, and Malky's house was as familiar to Bruchy as her own, and vice versa.

"Hi, Ma!" called Malky, "guess what!"

"What's up, Malky?" asked Mommy as she came in to the kitchen with a big smile. "Oh, Bruchy! Nice to see you. How are you?"

Bruchy answered first. "Mrs. Levine, we are just so excited. Malky and I were just chosen to be the class representatives to go to the Bais Yaakov convention this year."

"Well, *mazal tov*! Sounds great!"

"Mommy, it's better than great! Only two girls out of the whole school get to go!" explained Malky.

Bruchy continued. "To be chosen you had to have better than average grades, and participate in school projects. I think it was the *chesed* group that we organized on Sundays at the Harvest Home for the Aged that won us the trip."

"Maybe," said Malky. "Or maybe it was collecting the Chanuka gelt for girls in Russia?"

"Well, whatever it was, you're both very good students, and something that Emunah Academy can be proud of. I'm very happy for you both," said Mommy with a smile.

"But the best part," said Malky "is that the convention is being held in Evansville!"

Mommy dropped the laundry basket. "Well, that's pretty far, you know."

"Sure," said Bruchy. "Every year, another city gets to be the host. This year, it's Evansville's turn."

"Here I am in twelfth grade and I've never been on an airplane before," said Malky dreamily. "I am so excited!"

"Me too," said Bruchy. "I've never been past the Catskill mountains. Come on, Malky. Let's go tell my mother!"

"See you later, Mommy," called Malky over her shoulder. And off they flew, on their newly sprouted wings, happy as larks…. But singing larks don't always know what the weather will bring, and what will happen when they land.

★★★

Three weeks later, after much shopping and packing, instructions and planning, nerves and jitters, and just plain excitement, Malky and Bruchy stepped off the plane in Evansville's central airport. "I can't believe we're here!" squealed Bruchy, as she grabbed her luggage off the revolving carousel.

"Me neither," replied Malky, lugging her two large suitcases. "Look! There's the Evansville girl who's our hostess. She said she'd come to pick us up. See, she's holding a sign "Streicher -- Levine."

The girls quickly *shlepped* their stuff to their host. "Hi!" said the hostess. "I'm so happy you're here. My name is Sarah'la Friedman. Come on, I'll help with your stuff." As they walked out toward the car, Sarah'la turned to the girls. "So, which one of you is Streicher?"

"That's me. Bruchy Streicher."

"Which Streicher are you?"

"Oh, my father is from Williamsburg. So's my mother," said Bruchy.

"Really?! Say, did your mother come to the Evansville convention twenty-seven years ago in the snowstorm?"

"Yeah! She did! Since I was chosen to come, I must have heard that story told over eighteen times. How the snow began after they left town, how the bus skidded, how the entire 45 girls slept on the bus and then walked ten miles to the nearest gas station…"

"Wow! My mother's going to be so happy to meet you. She slept on that bus with your mother. When I heard the story, they walked fifteen miles to the gas station and only had water to drink…"

"But it was a good thing they had all that *nosh*…"

Sarah'la giggled, "Yes, that part of the story is the same. That's why wherever we go, we have to take food."

"Even to the mall," said Bruchy.

"Yep. Even to the mall. And which Levine are you?" Sarah'la asked, turning to Malky.

"Uh… I don't think I'm related to anyone you know," answered Malky slowly.

"Not the Levine from Camp Sosson?"

Malky shook her head.

"Or are you the Levine in the holocaust book I just read? The one who gave away his last piece of bread to…"

"No, I don't think so. Say, how far is the airport from your house?" Malky asked pointedly.

"We'll be there in fifteen minutes. If you look out this window, you'll see the cityscape of Evansville looming up in front of your eyes…"

★★★

"Welcome, welcome, girls," said Mrs. Shemtov, the principal of Bais Yaakov of Evansville, turning in every direction and smiling. "Can you believe that convention is finally here?" she asked rhetorically. "I am so glad to see you all nice and early on this *erev Shabbos*. First, I'd just like to make sure you each are wearing your name tag that should have come in your welcome kit." Groans filled the room. "I know it might feel *nebby*, but it's the greatest way to get to know each other, so please wear your name tag the entire time you're here in the *shul*. And, speaking of which, we called the first assembly for two o'clock in the afternoon so we can have a "Getting-to-Know-You" activity. Our Evansville girls have worked very hard to prepare this game. I'd like you all to give Breindy Sussman a warm welcome."

"Whoa! Evansville!" came an earth-shaking cheer, as Breindy rose from her seat. Yes, certainly the girls from Evansville were the biggest group, followed by a few other big cities. "Better, better, better, best! Bestway's the best!" came a counter cheer. "We're the lively, livewires from Livingston!" shouted another group. The room seemed to explode with shouts and songs.

Malky and Bruchy sat next to each other, looking around at so, so many other *frum* girls, from all around the country. "We don't have a cheer, do we?" asked Malky.

"No one would hear the two of us in the din anyhow. But this is really incredible," Bruchy said to Malky. "My grandmother would have tears in her eyes to see this. I would call her on my cell phone just so she could hear this noise, but it's probably almost *Shabbos* back in South Rover. My grandmother went through so much in her life. After the war, she couldn't believe she was lucky enough to survive and have a daughter to send to Bais Yaakov. That was my mother, you know."

"That really is something," murmured Malky.

"Yes, and my mother was an only child. But look. Now my grandmother even has married grandchildren and a great-grand-daughter who goes to Bais Yaakov."

"You mean your little kindergarten niece? Your married sister's daughter?"

"Yep. Fourth generation Bais Yaakov."

"Wow…" said Malky, her eyes glowing with awe.

The conversation was cut short by Breindy Sussman coughing loudly into the mike. She looked down at the paper which was slighting trembling in her hand. "Like, so… Right. So, wait a minute…" She glanced down at her paper. "Welcome to Evansville. We have a wonderful way of getting to know you. The game is called Family Tree. Here is the tree that we drew." Two girls from Evansville came forward and unrolled a huge mural sized paper. The renewed chanting and cheering from the Evansville classmates was silenced by Mrs. Shemtov's raised hand.

Breindy got over her initial stage-shyness and was herself by now. "Some girls at this convention already know that they're cousins." Girls smiled at their cousins. "Some girls are sister-in-laws." Sister-in-laws smiled. "And some girls are the aunt or niece of another girl here." Aunts and nieces smiled. "But a lot more of us are related in ways we don't even know. So, here at the bottom of the tree are three names, like three tree trunks." She turned and read the names, "Moishe and Freida Greenberg, Miriam and Mechel Rosenthal and Dina and Nosson Streicher. If anyone in the room is related to these people, they should come up and add their name to the family tree. Then, whoever is related to any of those girls can add their names. And then, well, you get the picture. In the end, we're pretty sure, that everyone in the room will be related to everyone somehow, and that shows how we're all one family. So, anyone who's related to the names I said, please come up and write your family onto the Bais Yaakov Convention Family Tree."

"Oh! I can't believe it," said Bruchy. "Dina and Nosson were my great-uncle and aunt. I'm so excited. I'll be back in a minute," and Bruchy made her way to the front of the auditorium, along with a score of other girls.

From her seat, Malky could see Bruchy laughing and hugging another girl. "You're my third cousin! I didn't even know!"

Amidst the noise, Breindy announced the names on the next layer of the tree, but Malky didn't hear them. She was already on her way outside to... well, to check on the weather at the corner of the block.

The Friday night *seuda* consisted of delicious *Shabbos* food and *zemiros*. "Isn't it funny? Even though we live so far away, I could tell you exactly what the menu would be half way across the country," said Malky. "*Challa,* gefilte fish, chicken soup, chicken with kugel... It's just like home."

"I don't know about your house, but mine's a lot quieter Friday night," said Bruchy with a laugh. "And that's *with* my little nieces and nephews."

Mrs. Shemtov stood up by her place by the head-table in the middle of the dining room with her hand raised. She waited for quiet. "Girls, since we don't have a microphone on Shabbos, you'll have to be very quiet for our first guest speaker. It is my pleasure to introduce to you Mrs. Raizy Ringold. Mrs. Ringold, as the Evansville girls know, was the founder of Bais Yaakov of Evansville forty years ago. In these forty years, the school has grown from the opening class of four girls in Mrs. Ringold's living room, to the thriving Bais Yaakov high school it is today, with three parallel classes in each grade."

"Whoa!! Evansvi...." The girls began, but then, when they glanced at Mrs. Shemtov's face, the cheer quickly dissipated.

"Thank you. Mrs. Ringold had three daughters in our school, and has, *baruch Hashem,* a number of granddaughters here now of whom we are very proud." A stern look at the Evansville tables kept the noise inside the lips "We have asked Mrs. Ringold to speak about her memories of Bais Yaakov and what it was like for her growing up in England. After the speech, we will divide up into workshops to discuss the round-table topic for this evening: the importance of *mesorah* and tradition in Bais Yaakov today. And now, Mrs. Ringold."

Mrs. Ringold slowly stood and walked to the head-table in the center of the room, escorted by a girl who was evidently a granddaughter. The girls blond hair was an echo of her grandmother's *sheitle.* She made sure her grandmother was sitting comfortably, and then went back to her own seat. At the end of the speech, a different granddaughter, one with an identical chin to her grandmother's, and a matching glowing smile, helped her back to her seat at the table.

Malky watched and sighed. Her grandmother would never be chosen to be a guest speaker at a Bais Yaakov convention, nor would she appreciate a noisy phone call on an *erev Shabbos*. She sighed, and took a bite of the predictable seven-layer cake. It was going to be a long *Shabbos*.

The ice cream bowls were emptied and the tablecloths held crumbs of the bagels that had been served at the gala *melave malka*. Left over, scattered sprinkles, and crumpled napkins attested to the fact that the evening's meal had been a grand success. The one-man-band was packing up his keyboard and the lights were dimmed. The girls rested in their chairs, tired from the dancing, contests, and excitement. It was 2:00 AM. Tomorrow would be the end of convention. What would tomorrow's event be?

Mrs. Shemtov rose and walked toward the microphone. She held the mike, looked around catching a number of girls eyes, smiling. "Girls, we have a special treat prepared for Sunday. Such a meeting has never yet occurred in the United States No one has ever had the opportunity to do this before, and you girls are the very first to have the privilege." There was some whispering, and shuffling. The girls faces looked expectantly toward the stage. What could this grand surprise be?

"We have here at the Evansville Bais Yaakov convention, a wonderful selection of girls from all around the country. It was an opportunity too good to be missed by some very important people from *Eretz Yisroel*. Tomorrow morning, starting at 9:00, a large number of representatives from different seminaries will be here to recruit students. Each of them arranged their schedules especially to meet with you and help you in your seminary decisions. Each of them will set up a booth, give out literature, and you'll be able to meet with them and discuss your plans."

Gasps and excited whispers filled the hall. Mrs. Shemtov held up her hand, waited for silence, and proceeded to speak. "I know, I know. You're not prepared for interviews, and your parents are not here to discuss the options. This is just an introductory meeting. There are many new seminaries opening, and this is your chance to get a feel for the programs. The seminary principals are just as eager to meet you as you are to meet them. Enjoy yourselves. After the meetings, a good-bye lunch will be served in the main hall. *Gut voch*, girls."

Chattering crowds of girls swirled toward the exit, with raised voices. "Wow! Pre-seminary interviews!" "I'm so excited." "I'm so scared." But the comment voiced most often among the entire group was, "I wonder if Rabbi Kopf from Bnos Tzlofchod will be here? Wouldn't *that* be unbelievable! Oh! I hope I can meet *him* tomorrow."

★★★

Bnos Tzlofchod. Even the name of the seminary conjured up images of wisdom, righteousness, and dedication, of young women who were learned, yet modest, proud, yet dignified. The line outside of Rabbi Kopf's cubby snaked around the entire auditorium and moved slowly forward. Someone from his staff stood answering the simplest questions, and then handed out cards with an Israeli phone number. Many girls were satisfied with walking away with a brochure and a smile. It was only the very interested and truly remarkable girls that stood for a very long time, waiting for a chance to meet the principal of this newly opened seminary and discuss the possibilities of spending a year in the environment of their dreams.

The line inched forward and at last Malky was directed to enter the cubby. Rabbi Kopf looked up from his desk and motioned to Malky to sit down. His bright green eyes sparkled behind his glasses, and his white beard flowed over his black jacket. "You're...?"

"Malky Levine." she replied.

"Which Levine is that?" he asked.

After an entire weekend of hearing the same question over and over again, Malky finally burst. She had had more than enough. Couldn't she just be judged on her own merits? What did her *family* have to do with anything at all? All the frustration of Friday and *Shabbos* came hurtling out onto poor Rabbi Kopf. "It's no Levine that you would know," said Malky, her loud voice grating on her own ears. "In fact, I'm down right tired of everyone asking me 'which Levine,' okay?"

"Why? Why are you so tired of it?" Rabbi Kopf asked quietly, his head tilted slightly.

"Why? *Why!?* Because I'm not related to anyone you know, okay? I'm not Rabbi Levine from South Gate's neice, and I'm not Mrs. Levine, the best teacher in Faircity's, granddaughter." She bit the words off viciously. "I'm not related to anyone famous, or special. My mother *wasn't* at the convention in Evansville twenty-five years ago and my father *didn't* study in yeshiva with anyone you know. No one wrote a book about them either. My parents are *baalei teshuva*, okay?"

"So?" asked Rabbi Kopf.

"So don't accept me into your seminary. I don't care!" Malky slumped back in the folding chair, her arms folded across her chest, tears welling up in her eyes.

"I'm sorry you seemed to have misunderstood my question," said Rabbi Kopf slowly. He leaned forward, speaking sincerely. "Asking about your family is not part of the admissions process. I ask that question to each girl just as an ice-breaker. Sometimes people feel comfortable speaking about something they know, like their family, before we get to reading a Ramban, or discussing which parts of *hilchos Shabbos* they've learned."

"Well I'm definitely not comfortable talking about my family," replied Malky heatedly.

"I don't see why not," insisted Rabbi Kopf. "Malky, you have to take a larger view of history. The *baalei beshuva* today are what the *chassidim* were less than two hundred years ago, and what the Hirschians were in Germany, and what the *perushim* were in the times of the *Gemara*. Do you understand?"

"Oh no, Rabbi Kopf. Those people were all important. My parents are just plain. Some people even... well, I've heard plenty people looking down on them like they're not good enough Jews."

"People looked down on *chassidim* too, and on any group that was loyal to Torah. It takes a lot of guts to go against the flow and it takes a while before the new movements are accepted into the mainstream. There was a time when it was hard for a *chassid* to find a *shidduch*... such was the lack of acceptance from family and community. In any case, you should be very proud of your parents."

"Proud?" asked Malky, her mouth practically dropped open. "I kind of try not to talk about them too much."

"I have the highest regard for *baalei teshuva*. I'm sure your parents are sincere," (Malky nodded her head) "dedicated to *Yiddishkeit*," (Malky nodded her head again), "and they must be doing something right if you're sitting here at the Bais Yaakov convention today." (Malky shyly hung her head).

"Malky Levine," Rabbi Kopf finished off, "*im yirtza Hashem*, when your parents are great-grandparents, your grandchildren will be able to brag about them. Your parents are the heroes that authors will write books about for the *next* generation."

The sincerity in Rabbi Kopf's voice, his open heart and open mind, struck a chord in Malky's heart. "Rabbi Kopf, I'm… I'm sorry about how I acted before. I actually think I would like to go to your seminary."

"And I'm sorry I offended you with my opening question," he replied. "Well then," he continued with a twinkle in his eye, flipping open the *chumash* on his desk, "onward with the Ramban."

Malky left the interview with Rabbi Kopf with hope in her heart. It was time to pack up her belongings that she had at her host's home, and get ready to say goodbye to Evansville and all the new friends she had met. She walked toward the door of the *shul*, looking for someone she knew to share the walk back to the house, when a new voice piped up.

"Hi! I didn't meet you yet. Where are you from?" A red-headed girl with freckles stood at her side trying to see the name tag still pinned to her sweater.

"Hi. I'm from South Rover. And you're from…." Malky squinted to read the girl's name tag.

"I'm from LA. My name is Frieda Molidsky. You know, from Molidsky's Ices? Oh, and I see your name is Malky Levine. Levine from Levine's Yeshiva? Was your mother in camp with my mother? Are you that Levine? I wonder if I know who your family is."

"Maybe you haven't heard our branch of the Levines. Maybe not yet. But someday," Malky said, with new-found self-assurance, "everyone will."

Listen
to the Weatherman

K ALMAN AND EZZIE SAT HUNCHED OVER THE CHESS BOARD. Kalman was nervous. His fingertip rested ever so lightly on the top of his rook. If he'd remove his finger, his move would be over and it would be Ezzie's turn, but he just wasn't sure if he wanted to give away his rook on the chance that he'd be able to capture Ezzie's queen in the next move. He sat in deep concentration, weighing the chances that Ezzie would even see the possibility of the queen escaping by moving his pawn forward rather than taking the rook.

Ezzie began to fidget. He took the last chocolate chip cookie from the plate and began to nibble.

"Shhhh," Kalman whispered, his brow furrowed.

Ezzie tried to chew quietly. He stared at the ceiling, at the books on the shelves lining the walls of Kalman's father's study, and at last at the clock. "Hey, Kalman!" he exclaimed. "It's already 9:00. *Maariv* starts in fifteen minutes. You want to finish the game this year?"

Kalman looked up, his finger still touching the rook. "I'm thinking Ezzie. It takes time to think, you know."

"I know, I know," Ezzie sighed, "but there's got to be a time limit. Just decide already… or I'm going home."

Kalman gave an exaggerated sigh and removed his finger. Ezzie quickly knocked off Kalman's rook with his queen. Kalman's eyes gleamed as he took Ezzie's queen with his knight.

He looked up at Ezzie with a grin. "You see why it takes time to move? You're always rushing. You should be more careful, you know…"

"Uh, huh," said Ezzie. He stretched his hand to the other side of the board and slid his bishop up close to Kalman's king. "Check mate. And next time, I'll try to be more careful."

Kalman's mouth dropped open. He looked at the board once more, and then swept the pieces off into the box. "Come on, then, it's time for *maariv*," he grumbled.

The boys stood and grabbed their jackets and hats. Ezzie took his winter jacket from the back of his chair and zipped it up. Kalman opened the door and was greeted by a cold burst of wind. "Bye, Ma," Kalman called to his mother, who was busy baking more cookies in the kitchen.

"Wear your winter coat," Ma called back. "I know you love the cold, but the temperature really dropped this evening."

"Okay, Ma," Kalman called as he pulled his coat out of the closet.

"Thank you for the cookies, Mrs. Shure," Ezzie added.

"My pleasure. Come again, Ezzie," Ma said.

The boys hurried down the block. Kalman glanced at Ezzie. "How'd you know to bring your winter coat? This morning when we left for yeshiva it was warm."

"I heard the temperature was supposed to drop tonight. Since we planned a chess game for after yeshiva and I figured a chess game at *your* house would take until *maariv*, so I took my coat already this morning."

In the darkness, Kalman looked at Ezzie with undisguised awe. "That was really smart," he said. "You'd be freezing otherwise."

"Yeah, well… You're not so dumb yourself," said Ezzie.

"I know, I know. But there's something about the way you think. See, I would have been embarrassed to walk into yeshiva with a coat in 50 degree weather. And look at the chess game. I thought for so long before moving, and you – you just zip in and win the game. What's your secret?"

Ezzie thought for a moment. "I guess I'm not so careful because I'm just not afraid of being wrong. Like, so what if I took my coat for nothing? So what if I loose the game?"

"Oh," said Kalman. "I like to be right."

"Well, I don't know if wanting to be right all the time is the best way to go," Ezzie replied.

Kalman shrugged. He prided himself in being right... if not always, then at least as often as humanly possible. Teachers knew they could rely on him to do well in every subject. Even on the ball field, he almost never missed a pitch. And if he did, even the sunniest summer day was blackened in his eyes. Why, ever since he was a little boy, he remembered the bright red 100%s that graced the top of his spelling tests. He was upset he lost that chess game, and could barely wait to play against Ezzie again – and win. He took being right very seriously.

The boys reached *shul, davened maariv*, and then each boy went back to his own home. Just as Kalman came in the door, the phone rang.

"Kalman, Ezzie's on the phone for you," his mother called. "You haven't spoken to him for a whole six minutes."

"Hi, Ezzie," said Kalman. He took off his glasses to wipe off the condensation, and then took a warm cookie from the tray. "Didn't run out of things to talk about yet?"

"Listen, Kalman. I just got home and my mother said she heard on the radio that there's going to be a storm tonight and school is going to be cancelled tomorrow."

"Great!" Kalman said. "Want to come over for a rematch? Only this time, you can't rush me."

"Better than that," said Ezzie. "If we can get up early in the morning and *daven hashkoma* at sunrise with my father, then we can go snow tubing up at Crystal Ridge for the day. My father has four-wheel drive on his jeep, so he's not afraid of snow. He said he can drop us off before he goes in to his office, and we'll probably be able to find a ride home. If not, he'll pick us up on the way home from work."

Kalman could hardly believe it. He loved snow tubing, and now that he was in *mesivta,* he hardly ever had enough time off to really enjoy the winter weather that he adored. To be the first boys out on the hills, before the crowds, would be exhilarating beyond words. There was also a lake next to the hills that offered ice skating and ice fishing, and a beautiful lodge, set up for visitors, with a fire burning in an old fashioned fire-place and huge stuffed bears standing guard by the doors. "Hold on a sec, Ezzie. I'll ask my mother."

He was back on the phone in a flash. "All's clear from here," he replied excitedly.

"Terrific," said Ezzie. "We'll be there to pick you up at 6:00 in the morning. Dress really warm, and bring food for the day. You think your mother has any more of those chocolate chip cookies?"

Kalman looked at the half-empty tray beside him and decided to pack up the rest before they disappeared. "Yep. Plenty more. I can bring sandwiches too, and we have thermoses for soup. We won't be hungry. And I'll bring a *sefer* along, so that we can learn something when we need to take a break. Thanks, Ezzie. This is the best thing that I could dream of!"

"See you tomorrow, then!"

"Bye."

★★★

It was before dawn when Ezzie's father's jeep honked in front of Kalman's house. Kalman came rushing out, dressed in a rugged, waterproof winter jacket instead of his black wool coat. On his hands he wore mittens – with gloves underneath – and on his feet he had mountain boots with wool lining. He lugged two backpacks, filled to the brim with food. A *sefer* peeked out of the outer zipper pocket.

He climbed into the car and pulled up his pants leg to show Dovid his long-thermals underneath. "Ready!" he said with a grin.

"Here we go! First stop – *shul*!" said Ezzie's father.

"Wait a second!" said Kalman. "I forgot my *tefillin*!"

In a flash, he flew into the house, and was back in the jeep, and the snow day began. After *davening*, Ezzie's father drove them up to Crystal Mountain, and dropped them off at the gate to the lodge. "Give me a call if you want me to come after work, okay? But I can't be here before five."

"Great!"

"Thanks!"

Ezzie and Kalman entered the lodge, walking under the neon flashing sign advertising 'a slidin' good time.' They were the first people at the desk, paid the fee for snow tubing, and signed away their lives as they initialed the safety waiver.

"About how often do people really get hurt?" Ezzie asked the man behind the counter as he directed them toward the colorful tubes.

"Did anyone ever die?" Kalman added nervously.

"Nah. No one ever gets hurt, and no one ever dies," said the man with a straight face. "Your tubes are over there. Enjoy the slopes."

Outside, the air was deliciously crisp. Kalman breathed deeply. It sure felt good to be outdoors, surrounded by nature. "It's so beautiful," he said. "I just hope that guy was right about not getting hurt!"

"Don't worry about it, Kalman. Look, they have twenty different lanes! This place has grown. Let's go!"

Ezzie grabbed his tube and flew down the first slope. Kalman sat down in his tube, grabbed the handles, and pushed off. As they flew, Ezzie laughed out loud! Snow flew into his mouth. He reached the bottom and was ready to do it again.

Kalman landed next to him a minute later. "Do you think I did it right? I have a feeling that I should be able to have a little more control over this tube. Like, there's practically no friction on the mountain. Maybe if I'd lean to the side, or maybe even weight down the back, I'd be able to steer, or at least regulate the speed."

Ezzie stared at Kalman. "Kalman. The joy of snow tubing is that there *is* no control. You just slide. That's why it's better than the old fashioned sledding. The chutes are made to be safe. Look, there are no trees, no fences. Just fun. Come on, Kalman. Try to enjoy."

The boys hitched a ride up the "Tow-Up-People-Mover" and rode back to the top of the hill. Down again! Up again! Down again! Up again! They raced through all the exciting runs, until, at last, their two hours were up and it was time to return the tubes.

"That was great!" Ezzie exclaimed. "It was worth coming early, when the slopes are empty. Did you notice we practically had the place to ourselves?"

"It couldn't have been better," Kalman agreed. "Let's go into the lodge. We can warm up and learn something."

The boys went in, peeled off their wet gear, and warmed their fingers and toes by the fire, and their hearts by the words of the *sefer* Kalman brought.

There was one other older man in the lodge who was renting skis. When he saw them take a break from their studies, he came over and introduced himself. "Hi. I'm Steve. Come here often?"

"Actually, neither of us has been here in a long time. We had a day off from school."

"Day off, eh? Well, enjoy. I actually come here all the time. I work as a safety volunteer and in return I ski for free. I never saw you guys before." Steve started putting on his gear – a belt loaded with all sorts of safety devices, rope, and a pocketknife. He gave the boys a brief explanation of what each item could be used for in case of emergency. "And these are my sunglasses," he said, sliding them onto his face.

"Sunglasses in the winter?" Kalman asked.

"Sure. By now, you realize that skiing is a big part of my life, right? Well, once I was skiing up in Alaska, and I got hit with snowblindness."

"Sounds bad," Ezzie said.

"Well, at the time, it was pretty scary. Snowblindness comes from UV rays reflecting off the bright snow. I had been out in the mountains on a very sunny day, and since I was sweating, and my goggles kept fogging up, I just removed them. Mistake. I woke up in the middle of the night in agony. My eyes kept tearing, and I couldn't see. Luckily, I was prepared. Covered my eyes with cool compresses for a day, and slowly I recovered."

"Wow. Didn't that make you want to quit skiing for good?" Kalman asked.

"Nah. If I let my mistakes get me down, I would have quit skiing at least six times. Let's see… once for each broken leg, once for getting stuck on the mountains during an all night blizzard, once for the frostbite… You get the picture."

The boys nodded.

"It's already lunch time," Kalman remarked. "We brought a lot of food. Want something to eat?"

"Nope," said Steve. "I never eat before I ski. Cramps, you know. It was nice meeting you guys. Enjoy the rest of your day." They watched him as he put on his boots, attached his skis, slid his sun-goggles over his eyes, and slowly stepped toward the slopes.

"Lunch time," Ezzie reminded Kalman, eying the backpack. They boys set up a small feast on the small wooden table next to their chairs and hungrily ate up everything. "You wouldn't want to have to *shlep* a heavy backpack home, right?" Ezzie laughed.

"That's for sure," Kalman said as he wiped his mouth on a napkin and glanced at his watch. "We still have time to go ice skating. You have enough money to rent skates?"

Ezzie nodded, and together they went down to the lake. "Size 10 and size 11 ½, please," Ezzie said.

"Here are your skates, sir," said a man wearing a ski cap and red, checkered jacket. "Some days we run out of those sizes. You're lucky."

"Yeah, looks like the lake has barely been touched," said Ezzie.

"You're the first customers today," the man in the ski cap said. "So watch out for soft spots." He glanced at Kalman's face. "You'll be a little safer sticking to the edges of the lake if you're scared, he ended kindly."

They enjoyed the skating, and then made their way back to the lodge and *davened mincha*. It didn't look like they'd be finding a ride home. Crystal Mountain was surprisingly empty. At last Ezzie called his father and they sat down to wait.

Ezzie's father arrived at 5:20. The boys were tired and impatient to get home and change into warm clothes. They rushed over to the jeep and climbed in.

"Hi boys. Sorry I couldn't come earlier. Once I get to work, I'm so busy, I can barely breath. You couldn't find a ride home with anyone else?"

"We didn't see anyone we knew," said Ezzie.

"Yeah. It's funny no one else came. I guess the kids from our *yeshiva* didn't think of it... or weren't lucky enough to have a ride," Kalman said. "We really had a blast."

"I'm happy for you." Ezzie's father made his way down the mountain. "Driving today is not really that bad," he said. "I'm not so sure they should have cancelled school."

As they drove back into town, they ran into traffic. There was slush on all the curbs and it began to drizzle. Trucks were moving slowly, and rush hour traffic was heavy,. Yellow school buses dotted the roads. Kalman looked out the window. "You know," he remarked, "it didn't snow that much after all."

A school bus stopped in front of the car, and they waited as the kids disembarked.

"Uh... guess what?" said Ezzie suddenly. "I think they *didn't* cancel school."

"Uh oh." Kalman's face paled in shock and he had a sinking feeling in his stomach. "You mean we *did* have yeshiva today?"

"Certainly does seem like it," said Ezzie slowly. "The kids getting off that bus are in our class."

"We skipped!" gasped Kalman. "We spent the day snow tubing and skating when we should have been in school. Boy, are we going to be in trouble."

"Well, at least now we know why no one else was on the slopes," Ezzie laughed.

"How can you laugh?" Kalman groaned.

"Hey, Kalman, take it easy. It was a mistake," Ezzie said calmly.

"Mistake! I'll say! A big one! And it was your fault," he said accusingly to Ezzie.

"So what? Everyone makes mistakes."

Kalman just stared. "I don't. I mean, I try not to."

Ezzie just shrugged. The car pulled up to Kalman's house, and Kalman climbed out. Ezzie looked at Kalman's face. Gone was the carefree grin, the wind blown, reddened cheeks, and happy sparkle in his eye. It was replaced by the intense, nervous "I-have-to-always-be-right" look he recognized from the chess game. "Try to take it easy, Kalman. See you tomorrow in Yeshiva… probably in the Rosh Yeshiva's office."

Kalman just sighed, and, head low, went into his house, his empty backpacks slung sadlyl over his shoulder.

Sure enough, the next morning found the two hooky-players waiting for the Rosh Yeshiva after *shachris*. But, surprisingly – to Kalman especially – the meeting went very well. "Looks like you boys counted your chickens before they hatched," the Rosh Yeshiva said. "Next time, make sure yeshiva is really cancelled before you decide to take the day off. I'm sure you learned some Torah during the day, right?"

They nodded. Ezzie was lucky that Kalman was his friend.

"All right, then. Go ahead back to class, and try not to make the other boys jealous with stories about your antics."

Kalman stopped Ezzie outside the door of the classroom. "I

guess you were right, Ezzie. Sorry I got so upset yesterday after we had such a nice time. It's just that I hate making mistakes."

"I know. Maybe it's because you're the *bechor* in your family that you try so hard. But no one is perfect."

"Wait a minute, Ezzie! You're also the oldest in your family. How come you know how to take it so easy? Who taught you?"

Ezzie looked down for a second, and then replied, "I used to be afraid of being wrong, too. But I changed because of the weatherman on the radio."

"What does *that* mean?"

"You ever listen to the radio? Whenever we get into the car to drive somewhere, my mother or father flips on the radio to hear to weather and traffic." Ezzie put on a deep voice, imitating a radio announcer. "This is your weather report: Tomorrow, heavy clouds will move into the area. There will be 6-8 inches of snow in the city. North and west of the city, there will be 10-12 inches, followed by a freezing rain. Rush hour traffic will be severe. The weekend weather will follow after this announcement."

Ezzie reverted back to his regular voice. "See, they get you hooked. You have to listen to this dumb commercial about stuff that will make you grow hair if you're bald, or people who will invest your money for you. The advertisers pay a lot of money to have their ad squished into the weather report where they know you'll listen. After the paid announcements, the weatherman comes back on:"

His voice dropped a pitch. "Two days from now will be unseasonably warm. Eastern winds from the ocean will bring relief from the storm. Over the weekend, clear skies and lingering humidity. And now for the traffic…."

Ezzie laughed. "But you know, even after a report like that, the snow might never come, or it maybe there will be just a few flakes. The storm might come, instead, over the week-end. The funniest thing is that, even if he was totally wrong, the same guy is on the radio with all sorts of other predictions the very next day, And he never apologies. He never says, 'I'm really sorry for all those folks who had expensive week-end plans because I said there would be nice weather and then they had to cancel because the airports were closed.' Nope. He just keeps on guessing at the weather day after day, and never loses his job.

"After listening to this for quite a while, it dawned on me that I might as well act like the weatherman. Lots of times I guess at things. Sometimes I'm right. And if I'm not, so what? I'll just go on guessing the next time."

The boys went into class and opened their *gemaras*, but Kalman couldn't stop thinking about what Ezzie had told him. He always tried so hard to be right --- about everything. Maybe it really didn't matter if he was right all the time. Even the Rosh Yeshiva had been casual about his mistake.

He thought about the countless nights he had lost sleep, worrying about tests, worrying about making a mistake. Perhaps things could change. Suddenly, his Rebbe's voice broke into his day dream. "Kalman, why do you think Rashi brings down this *passuk* here instead of back on *Daf gimel*?"

Kalman looked up. Usually, he'd be shaking if he didn't know the answer, but today, something had changed. "I'm sorry, Rebbe," he said quietly. "I wasn't paying attention."

"All right," said the Rebbe, "try to space in. Moishe, do you know why Rashi said…"

Suddenly Kalman felt as if wings were sprouting on his back. He could soar like a bird above his worries. He was free! So what if he didn't know every answer? It was time to learn to loosen up, enjoy learning, and enjoy life, without the nervous tension he had carried around since his childhood.

And maybe… just maybe, he'd become a weatherman when he grew up. Then it wouldn't make the slightest difference to anyone -- ever -- whether he was right or wrong.

QWERTY

"ARENʼT YOU SUPPOSED TO GO FASTER THAT THAT?" Chana asked, leaning over her sister's shoulder as she typed on the computer in the paneled study. "When Mommy types, her fingers fly. Your fingers look like they're glued to the keys."

"My fingers are confused," Ruchy snarled, rebuffing her little sister's approach. "I'm in high school now, you know. I'm under a lot of pressure. Don't you have anything else you have to do?"

"You needn't be so brusque," Chana replied with a shrug. "I just came by to bring you some fresh peanut butter cookies I baked."

Ruchy leaned back in her chair and relaxed for a moment, letting the tension of her task slip from her shoulders. She took a cookie and bit into it, enjoying the sweet taste. "Thanks, Chana. Sorry for being 'brusque.' That's a pretty good word for an eighth grader. Where'd you pick it up?"

"It's from this week's vocabulary test," she said smugly. "We get points if we find the words in print and bring them into class, and we're supposed to use them in real conversation so they become part of us. Emulate, evoke, inaugurate, pervade…"

Ruchy grimaced. "Enough, enough!" she said, covering her ears. "I just wish *I* could go back to the good old days of elementary school, where all we did was take vocabulary tests, practice handwriting and bake cookies. After years of learning to form beautiful, fluid script, look what they've done to us! All that hard work is thrown aside in favor of the dull type of this gruesome machine."

She took another cookie and continued. "I'm not the only one who feels like this. The whole ninth grade is suffering. Every day we march into Mrs. Concise's classroom and listen to her chant 'a-s-d-f-g-h-j-k-l-;-' enter.' She's the meanest, strictest teacher in the universe and she actually expects our fingers to hit the right keys! Soon all our reports will have to be typed! I don't think I'll ever be able keep up!

"And just look at this crazy keyboard!" Ruchy continued. Chana looked at the keyboard, not sure quite what she was supposed to see or say, but nodding sympathetically at her older sister's pain. "Why in the world didn't they just line up the keys in the order of the A-B-C's? What a mess! And we're supposed to learn to touch-type without looking at our fingers? How will I ever find the letters without peeking?"

"At least the numbers are in the right order," Chana volunteered hopefully, pointing to the top line.

"Doesn't help," Ruchy complained. "When we type lots of numbers, we use the keypad on the right side, which is arranged in the *upside-down order* of a telephone keypad. I'm telling you, Chana: some despicable people out there are trying to make my life miserable. This typing practice is excruciating. I hate typing," she concluded, folding her arms and frowning at the keyboard in silence.

The silence was suddenly broken by a squeaky, screeching sound down the hall. Ruchy jumped. "What was that?" she asked.

"Sorry. You weren't home this afternoon. I should have warned you," Chana replied.

"What is it? Is the washing machine broken?"

The shriek blasted again, this time closer. Ruchy looked under her desk. "I hope the computer isn't going to explode. What is it? An air raid siren?" Then she saw Chana laughing. "What's so funny about that awful sound?"

At that moment, the door to the study flew open. In walked their little sister Esty, holding a small flute and blowing as hard as she could.

"Ow! My ears!" cried Ruchy. "That's deafening!" She gingerly pulled the instrument from Esty's hands.

"Hey! Give it back! It's my new recorder! We just got it today in music! Give it back, Ruchy," Esty cried, stamping her foot. "I have to practice. My teacher said so. My teacher says it just takes practice. And my teacher said that by Chanuka we'll all be able to play the *dreidle* song. And my teacher says…"

"O-U-T!" cried Ruchy . "Did your teacher tell you what that spells? Out! Out now!" She held out the recorder, pointing toward the door.

"And my teacher says," Esty mumbled on her way out the door, grabbing back the recorder, "not to give up."

Ever resilient, Esty went back to her music, putting her little fingers on and off the small holes as she walked down the hall. Over and over. And over…

"Oh, bother," complained Ruchy from behind the closed door. "And I have to learn to type with background music! Life is so hard!"

"Do not succumb to such turbulent emotions," replied Chana, holding out another cookie and a cup of milk. "Drink before you dehydrate."

"And you! Get out of here with your eighth grade words and let me be miserable in peace."

Ruchy not-so-gently escorted her sister through the door, but not before Chana pointed out that a 'miserable peace' is an oxymoron. The Ruchy slumped down at the keyboard to finish her snack and contemplate the wretched endeavor before her.

t…t…f…f..g…g..v…v…b…v…That one finger on her left

hand had an awful lot of work to do. "I quit!" she finally cried. "This is the most demeaning thing I've ever tried. I'm good at math, I'm good at science, I can sing, I can dance, I can even make better cookies than Chana – but I never have been so stumped! Oh, you cruel computer," she sobbed, and hit the off button, taking away its electric life support and killing it -- for the moment.

She got up to leave, and then returned to the scene of the crime, pausing for a moment to look at the cadaver before leaving the study. She gave a cursory glance at the keyboard, and then looked more closely. Then she decided to take inventory, and began to count the letters.

Ha! Just as she suspected. The twenty-six letters of the alphabet were distributed in a lopsided way. Her left hand was burdened by having to reach a total of fifteen letters, while her right hand, the one that was certainly more adept, was only given eleven letters, plus the commas, periods and quotation marks! No wonder she was having such a ridiculously hard time mastering this skill!

She sat back and contemplated the bleak situation. Something had to change… It was crazy to think that any intelligent person could be subjected to a year of typing practice, followed by a lifetime of such nonsense…

Then it dawned on her. Something could change -- Something *would* change! She would make a new keyboard! She would place the letters in some kind of order -- something more sensible than this hodge-podge, something logical, and easy to learn. If everyone in the world had to learn to type, she could make a fortune! The more she thought about it, the more excited she became.

She turned off the light and slowly went upstairs to bed, her mind racing with the prospects. She would need to collaborate with someone, an adult who know how to get things done, and together they would electrify the world with their discovery! But who? Who could help?

The answer was so obvious that she laughed aloud. Of course! It had to be the mirthless Mrs. Concise, her typing teacher! She knew almost everything about typing! She'd been announcing those same letters, unsmiling, for so many years, torturing class after class of students. She'd be the first one to agree that there was a need for a solution – and such a brilliant solution, at that.

Late at night, as she lay in bed, she dreamed of marketing her new product to computer manufactures around the world. And as she drifted off to sleep, she even allowed herself to imagine how she would spend her millions...

She woke up in the morning to a strange song. She thought it was the keyboard coming to haunt her, until she realized it was just Esty, singing at the top of her lungs. "G-G-A-A-B-G..." she sang.

"That's not '*Modeh Ani*'" Ruchy complained. "What in the world are you singing?"

"That's the notes for *dreidle, dreidle, dreidle*," Esty explained. "Mommy took my recorder last night because she said I shouldn't play in the dark."

"Humph. There might be more reasons she took it away than that," Ruchy muttered as she climbed out of bed.

"So I'm practicing just the names of the notes. B-D-D-C-B-A-" She continued singing as she put on her shoes and skipped downstairs. "Mommy! Where's my recorder?"

In a few minutes, Ruchy, Chana and Esty were sitting around the table, clad in their uniforms, polishing off the prior night's cookies, before starting breakfast in earnest. Ruchy ate a bowl of cereal quickly, stopping only to grab the recorder out of Esty's hands.

"But my teacher said the more we practice the better it is!" she protested.

"Your teacher wants you to eat breakfast, so your fingers will be nice and strong," Ruchy said firmly. "No playing during meals."

The girls left for school together. As Ruchy walked past the computer in the study, she turned to glance at the keyboard. It seemed to taunt her. "Ha! Can't learn to type. There's the girl who can't learn type!" She shook her fist at the machine. "Pipe down, dumb machine. Wait until we rip your little keys off and rearrange them logically! You may have defeated me in battle last night, but we'll see who wins the war."

The morning seemed to drag by. Finally it was time for English studies. Ruchy's friends were surprised, even shocked, at her enthusiasm, as she ran to be on time for typing class.

That day, she was the first student sitting at her computer, her fingers resting patiently on the keys. She diligently struggled to behave and make a good impression on Mrs. Concise – for the first time – knowing that she had a big favor to ask her at the end of the class. Finally, the bell rang, and she rushed over to catch the teacher.

"Mrs. Concise?"

"Yes?" Mrs. Concise peered at the eager student in surprise. The first week of school, she was often surrounded by students. They begged to be excused from typing, claiming it was 'so hard,' that they had to 'help their mothers at home,' that there was 'too much homework' and they'd 'never be able to learn.' But once the girls realized there was no escape, and she made a point of emphasizing over and over how typing was a skill they would need in life, they settled down for the daily practice sessions. And in the end, they did all learn. Some faster and some slower, but yes, by the end of the year, even the most stubborn resisters learned to type.

"Mrs. Concise, I have an idea," Ruchy continued.

"An idea?" Typing was not for ideas. She stood, arms crossed, waiting to see the doctor's note, excusing her student from typing for the semester, due to a sprained muscle in her pinky.

Ruchy sidled over to her, and looked furtively around. "I don't want anyone to hear," she explained.

Mrs. Concise's eyebrows rose in surprise.

"It's like this. I have a plan to make millions. And I'd like to invite you to be a part of it."

Mrs. Concise glanced at her student sideways, and reached for the cell-phone in her pocketbook. Something was wrong.

"No, no. Don't worry, Mrs. Concise," Ruchy reassured her. She took a breath. Her teacher thought she was nuts, she quickly surmised. Better get to the point. "I had a brilliant idea last night, an idea that will revolutionize the world."

Mrs. Concise held the phone, clearly trying to decide who to call for help.

"The problem is the keyboard, Mrs. Concise. It makes no sense. All we have to do is rearrange the keys logically, and we can manufacture a smart product. Anyone will be able to learn if the keys are set up right. I mean, shouldn't the right hand do more typing than the left hand since most people are righties? And shouldn't the letters that are used most often be easier to reach? Shouldn't the vowels all be in one corner, and the unimportant letters be placed low down in hard to reach spots? Shouldn't..."

She paused and noticed that Mrs. Concise was smiling. Ruchy hardly recognized the ancient face wrinkled up in a smile. "Well? What do you think? I figured I'd share the profits with you – like maybe 40%-60%? I mean it's my idea and all, but you'd have to do all the grown up stuff like applying for a patent."

Mrs. Concise's smile widened. "My dear. You are right on all counts. You are right that the QWERTY keyboard makes no sense."

"QWERTY?"

"It's called that because those are the first six letters on the left hand. And you're right that it's illogical. It was set up that way because on old typewriters, the main thing was to make sure when the keys were hit, the little metal bars that tapped the ink to print on the paper shouldn't jam together. The designer made sure that the letters typed most often in sequence should be operated by opposite hands. For example, "th" is a very common blend. That's why the "t" is typed by the left hand and the "h" is typed by the right. Nowadays, with computers, there are no little metal bars, and yes, they have developed more logical keyboards. Professor Dvorak, for example, set up a keyboard which has five vowels and the five most common constants in the home row where your fingers rest."

Ruchy's shoulder's slumped. "But… but then why don't we learn Dvorak's system?"

"Because even though it makes more sense, all the research in the world didn't prove that a more logical keyboard resulted in faster typing. Fast typists type fast, and slow ones type slow. Typing isn't driven by thought. It's just training. All it takes to learn is practice, practice, and more practice. Why should the whole industry turn over, why should all the equipment change, why should all typists be retrained if it doesn't make a difference?"

Ruchy sighed. She stood speechless, feeling like she had been run over by a truck.

"Don't worry, dear," said Mrs. Concise. "You too will learn to type QWERTY. They all do. And with your brains, I'm sure you'll accomplish something more important in your life than modifying the keyboard." And with that, Mrs. Concise returned her phone to her pocketbook, and her smile to wherever it had been stored, and wished Ruchy a good day.

The cold weather came, and with it, Chanuka. To the surprise and amazement of the entire family, when they sat down to eat the first latkes, Esty played *dreidle, dreidle, dreidle*, in clear, recognizable, flawless notes.

Chana and Ruchy applauded.

"I derived great pleasure from that song," said Chana in her eighth grade way.

"Wow!" said Ruchy. "How'd you do it?! You're brilliant! That was awesome!"

"My teacher said you don't have to be brilliant, Ruchy," Esty explained calmly. "My fingers just learned it without me." And with that, Esty began her performance again.

And again. And again. And…

"Uh, maybe that's enough," said Ruchy.

"You want a turn?" Esty asked. "It works on the piano too! My teacher said."

"What if I just type the notes instead?" said Ruchy. And, with a flick of the switch, the computer returned to life, and the sisters played a duet. Ruchy typed the notes on the keyboard, while Esty sang along:

G-G-A-A-B-G
B-D-D-C-B-A
A-A-B-B-C-A
A-D-C-B-A-F
D-B-D-B-D-B.
G-G-A-A-B-G
B-D-D-C-B-A
A-A-B-B-C-A
A-D-C-B-A-G

(To readers: These are the real notes. You can play along too!)

Trouble on the Ranch

"H ungry?" Asher asked Levy on their way out of class.
"What a question! Of course, I'm hungry. I'm starving."
Levy pressed his hand to his stomach and pretended to be falling over.

"I figured. It's part of becoming *bar mitzva*," said Asher. "So you want to come with me to my brother's restaurant for something to eat on the way home?"

Levy's eyes lit up. Everyone knew that Asher's brother's restaurant had the best hamburgers in town. "I'd love to," Levy replied, "but..." He pulled out the lining of his pockets. "I'm broke."

"Don't worry," said Asher. "My brother's a generous guy. When he sees how hungry we are, and how we barely have enough energy to stumble through the door, he'll feed us."

"Great," said Levy. "But remember: I got permission from my mother to go to the class genius' house after yeshiva to study for the *gemara* test, so we can't stay too long."

"Thanks for the compliment," Asher laughed. "Come on, then. Let's go."

The boys arrived at a glass door emblazoned with the bright red logo of "Z's Ranch," in the shape of a cowboy hat. Pushing open the swinging door, they had to squirm their way through the crowds to the front of the store. On the walls, there were life-sized photos of cowboy ranches and fields, cows and horses. Strung over the doorways were lassos, and the tables were made out of a rustic type of wood. Walking into Z's was like walking into another world.

Behind the counter stood a tall man wearing a red cowboy hat with a feather.

"Howdy, Asher! What a treat! Folks, this is my little brother Asher." The half dozen men sitting at the wooden counter all nodded a greeting between bites. "So you found some time to peek out of your *gemara* and come to visit your big brother, eh? Who's your friend?"

"This is Levy. Levy, this is Z."

"Z?"

"Short for Zelig," Z laughed. "Shneur Zelig Zalman was too hard for my many friends to pronounce."

"You bet. Only easy names for me," said one man. He wiped his lips, and pushed his chair back. "Great steak, Z. I'm only leaving to make space for the next customer. Nice seeing you."

"See you, Mr. Przewozbornski."

Within a minute, the vacant seat was filled by a new customer, who placed an order for a "Z Burger" and fries. Z shouted the order back to the kitchen, and then commented on the man's nice hat, getting details about where he bought it and which colors were available.

Within the few minutes it took the boys to admire the fresh selection of foods, they saw many customers come, choose a meal or snack, and leave with a smile and a friendly word from Z. He gave an extra cookie to a toddler, and carried a large cold cut platter to the table for a woman with a huge crew of kids. He personally rushed to open the exit door for a man with a walker, and carefully escorted him to the waiting car.

"That was Mr. Silver," he explained to Asher. "Comes every day for a cup of Z's coffee and a serving of hot sauce that he adds to whatever lunch they bring him from the meal delivery program. Doll of a man. And here's Mrs. Cohen! Ah! Mrs. Cohen! *Mazal tov* on the new baby. Cute little one, just like his brothers."

The group of Cohen boys smiled shyly. "Here's your Thursday chicken crisps," he announced, and he seated them at a table where the chairs were shaped like little horses. Then he was in motion once again, taking orders, pouring drinks, and always smiling.

Asher and Levy watched the action and excitement. "Your brother really built up a great place here," Levy commented. "I'd love to stay all night, but, Asher... the *gemara*.."

"Okay, so let's order." They went over to the counter to speak to Z about a "brotherly discount." Just then, the door flew open and the mail carrier walked in. "Hi, Z," he said with a friendly wave. "Any donuts left over from yesterday?"

"Here you go, Russ," Z said, handing him a bag from below the counter with a smile. "And what have you got for me?"

"Today's mail. This one is certified. You've got to sign for it," the mail carrier said, handing him a pen.

Z took it and scribbled his initials on the form, and wished the mail carrier a good day. Then he took the envelope and tossed it somewhere behind the counter.

"Aren't you going to open it, Z?" asked Asher.

"Open it? Are you kidding? There's a lot more than that one unopened envelope, little brother." Z motioned to Asher to come behind the counter. "What do you think of that? A whole laundry basketful."

Asher's eyes bulged in astonishment.

"Hey, at least I didn't throw it all away," Z said defensively. "I'm pretty busy, you know. I figure I'll get to it some day, but how would I ever have time to make new recipes, or money, if I were busy opening all those envelopes? Now, what would you growing boys like to eat?"

"Uh, what can we get for free?"

"Two burgers coming up," Z said, and he reached into his cash register. "Here's some quarters. Go buy yourselves soda too."

Asher and Levy maneuvered their way through the crowded eatery. "You know, I would never have guessed that Z is your brother," Levy said after they washed, said *hamotzie*, and squeezed into an empty table to eat. "You speak in words, he speaks in whole paragraphs. You're short and skinny, he's so big and... well, I guess if you work around food all day, that's what happens. You're on the quiet side and serious, but your brother-- he must know the whole town! The only thing you have in common is that you wear the same glasses," Levy concluded.

"He picked them out for me. The list goes on and on. He takes risks, I'm a scaredy cat. He hated school and never really learned to read, while learning is just about my favorite thing to do in the whole world." Asher said.

"You're Mr. Books."

"I know. And he's Mr. Street-Smarts. But when all is said and done, we're still brothers, and I like his food." Asher fiddled with his napkin. "I just hope all that unopened mail doesn't get him into trouble."

"Why don't you volunteer to read it for him?"

Asher looked at Levy. "That's brilliant. I didn't think of it. I would love to help him out. If he'll let me, I'll do it!"

The boys finished their meal and, on the way out, Asher presented his offer to Z.

"Consider it a deal," Z said, pulling out the basket. "Read it, sort it, have fun, and save me any good credit card offers. Can you carry the basket? It's heavy."

The boys each took one handle, and then nodded.

"Have a nice walk home then," Z waved. "By next month, I hope I'll be able to offer you a ride!"

"What did he mean 'offer us a ride'?" panted Levy, already out of breath from the weight of the basket.

"He has his eye on a Jeep," Asher explained. "He's been saving for it since he opened the business two years ago. Goes with his image. It sounds like he finally saved enough money to buy it. Wow. This is heavy. One more house and we're there."

The boys finally pushed open the front door and *shlepped* the basket up the steps to Asher's room. "Ready to learn?" asked Asher.

"Sure. But maybe you should just open that one letter Z signed for. Not all mail comes certified. Maybe it's important."

"Good idea. Let's see." Asher read the return address aloud "'New York Department of Taxation and Finance' Uh oh. This sounds serious." He tore open the envelope and read under his breath: *The said county, town, village or municipal corporation from a part of the whole thereof; and in case of a judgment, the court may, in its discretion, vacate, set aside and open said judgment, with leave and direction for the defendant therein...* blah, blah, blah... *enforce any existing legal or equitable defense therein under the direction of such personas the officer having the custody thereof...* blah, blah, blah... *action now existing to be liable to pay tax...*

"No wonder Z doesn't read this stuff. But look at this, Levy. On the bottom it says that the tax compliance division is going to show up tomorrow at Z's. Oh no! And if he doesn't pay his back taxes within five days, they'll send police officers! Poor Z!"

Levy grabbed the letter and read it. "Quick. Let's look through the laundry basket for other letters from the government!"

Sure enough, amidst advertisements for kitchen equipment, foreign vacations and telephone plans, there were tens of letters bearing the same return address.

"We showed up in the store just in time," Levy finally said. "This is serious. You'd better warn your brother."

Asher paced back and forth, wiped the sweat off his forehead, picked up the phone, and dialed Z's Ranch.

"Hi... uh, Z. Is that you? Uh...it's Asher. Yeah, the food was great. Uh, listen... uh... I have some, uh, not-so-good news for you." He cleared his throat.

"Look Asher," said Z, above the background noise. "I'm kind of busy, you know. It's dinner time and the place is cookin'. You called about something specific?"

"Well, uh… You might be in a little bit of trouble with this mail that you… uh… that got neglected."

"Uh, huh. Burger to go?" he shouted to a customer. "Listen, Asher. You're the smart brother. So get me out of the trouble, okay? Write whatever letters you have to and come by for me to sign 'em. Any credit card offers?"

"Uh, I didn't see any," Asher said.

"Okay then. So maybe I'll see you later… Six sodas? Be with you in a sec. Thanks, little brother. Bye."

Asher put down the phone and shook his head. "You heard that? I should write some letters and solve his problems! I'm only thirteen. What do I know about business problems? You think I should tell my parents? I just would hate to take away any *nachas* from them. They're finally happy about how Z's turning out."

"You know," said Levy, "my father has been running a business for years."

"No wonder you caught on to this right away."

"Yep. I've heard people call him lots of times for advice. You mind if I use your phone? I'll ask him if he can stop into Z's on the way home from work."

Levy explained to the situation to his father and arrangements were quickly made. "My father said to bring all the relevant mail and he'll pick us up in fifteen minutes. We'll have to drag Z away from the counter and explain the threat hanging over his neck."

"Z," said Asher when they walked through the swinging ranch door for the second time that evening. "This is Mr. Strateman, Levy's father."

"Hello, and so nice to meet you. And how can I help you? Fried beef dish? Spicy fries? You look like a *parve* milk shake man. How 'bout vanilla?"

"I'm afraid the boys brought me here to help *you*," Mr. Strateman said.

Asher grabbed Z's right elbow and Levy took the left, and they steered him to a table in the back of the store.

"Perhaps you should sit down," suggested Mr. Strateman.

"Wha- what's going on? I can't sit down now. I never sit down during work," Z protested.

It was a struggle to get him to listen, but once he did, Z asked one of his cooks to take over the counter and he sank into a chair. "But I didn't do it on purpose. Honestly. It never occurred to me."

Mr. Strateman stared at Z. "What do you mean? It never occurred to you to pay taxes? Who doesn't know about paying taxes?"

"I guess I don't. Look, I never listened much in school. Isn't that the truth, Asher?"

Asher nodded. "Yeah, but I don't think they even teach us about taxes in school."

"It's a shame," said Mr. Strateman.

"Well, even if they did, I would have missed it," Z admitted. "I used to run home to make hotdogs during English and then bring them back in time for *mincha* to sell to my friends. My hobby evolved into a business. My father's friend owned an empty storefront and he liked me, so he gave me the space and set me up in business. In exchange, I cater his *simchos* for free. That's all I know about business. Maybe this is all just a joke?"

"I hate to be the one to tell you, but this is for real. You already received a tax-warrant," he held up one paper for Z to see, "which creates a lien against your property. That means you probably won't be able to borrow any money. Have you tried to get any business loans lately?"

"No business loans, but I was wondering why I couldn't get a car loan. Ah well. It doesn't matter. I already have nearly enough money saved up to buy the car outright." He breathed a sigh of relief.

"The state hasn't threatened to take money out of your bank account?"

"What bank account? I save all my money in shoe boxes. Hey! Don't laugh," Z protested, looking at the faces surrounding him. "Look. I never learned about any of this stuff. I'm not the scholarly type. You can ask anyone. Just tell me,what do I do now?" Z said, looking helplessly at Mr. Strateman.

"Look, Z. At this point, the state can levy your property. That means if you had your money in the bank, they could take it. If you already had the car, they could take it away. Instead, they'll probably do a seizure and sale, like it says in this letter." He held up another paper that Z had ignored.

"Go ahead. Tell me what that means," he said, slumping further down in his seat.

"The state will send a tax compliance agent to your business, dump out the money from your cash register, and padlock the doors. Then they'll sell all your stuff at an auction and use the money to pay your tax bill."

Z gasped. He looked around the restaurant. "Destroy Z's? You mean… you mean they'd sell my horse chairs and tables? My refrigerators? My deep friers? My artwork? The lighting? My staff's custom-made, matching cowboy hats? I worked so hard to build up this business. Do you think there's any chance to save my store? I'd do just about anything to hold on to The Ranch. It's my life."

He looked like he was near tears. Asher and Levy felt so bad for him. He was such a nice guy, after all, and hadn't *meant* any harm.

"You could try to find a lawyer, but it's really late." He glanced at his watch. "Offices are already closed for the day. My advice would be to pay up tomorrow when they come around. You can work out a payment plan with them, but of course, until the amount is paid up, you'll be paying interest on the balance and penalties." He flipped through the piles of papers back and forth and then said, "This is the amount due. The faster you pay, the less you'll owe. Do you think you could come up with this much money?" he asked, pointing to a fee at the bottom of the page.

Z looked so pathetic, hoping against hope. "There's no escaping? You think maybe if I ignore the letters, they'll go away?"

"Death and taxes. There's no escape."

"Good-bye Jeep?" sighed Z.

"I'm afraid so," Mr. Strateman said. "My last bit of advice, Z, if you want to hear…?"

"Yes?"

"If you don't want to worry about the business part of the business, find an honest accountant – like my accountant, David -- who will keep track of all this for you. What you have to do is make sure to give him the mail, and listen to him. Hiring him and then ignoring his advice isn't going to help much."

"Well then, so be it," said Z, standing. "Can you ask your David to give me a call? I guess this is all part of running a business. Hey, Asher! Don't look so sad, little brother! You and Levy are the heroes in this story. You saved my store. And I'm going to get that Jeep. You'll see. It'll take a little more time, that's all.

Z's face suddenly lit up. "But I have a new idea! Maybe I should do work for the government! With the amount of taxes I'll be paying, and everyone else pays, I'll bet they have a whole lot of money to spend. Maybe I should start making hamburgers for state employees, or maybe I should offer to serve hot lunches in the state capitol during their endless meetings. Maybe I'll open another branch of Z's close to the courthouse. Hey, maybe I can even work out a contract with the military to provide Z-burgers to the troops. Now that's a way to make money! I'm going to start looking for investors right now."

Mr. Strateman laughed. "Keep me in mind," he said as he stood up. "I can see that you'll be a success."

Z wiped off a bit of stray ketchup from his hands, and with his characteristic grin shook Mr. Strateman hand and walked him to the door, thanking him profusely. Then he practically ran back to his place behind the counter calling, "Who's waiting to order?

And who's looking to invest in a great new business? Line starts here. Free soda for the first twenty investors...."

Asher and Levy stood up. "Back to the *gemara* for us," said Levy. And with their stomachs still full from dinner and their hearts full of satisfaction, having helped a fellow Jew, they left the Ranch, and returned to the world of Torah.

Fog

OG SWIRLED AROUND THE GREYHOUND BUS as it sped along Route 95 through New England. The road was only visible for a few hundred feet ahead, and beyond the barriers stretched what looked like a huge, endless sea of grey. The highway signs were blurred, and there was a muffled feeling of emptiness over the whole landscape that was broken only by the thin arc of asphalt that stretched southward. When the bus pulled into New Haven, and Yitzy looked up from the *chumash* he was learning, he could barely see the street lights on the side of the road struggling to illuminate the pervasive greyness.

A handful of passengers climbed onto the bus and found seats. "Good thing the driver knows his way," a man commented as he sat down next to Yitzy.

Yitzy smiled and nodded. He looked back into his *sefer*, and then glanced at his watch. An hour more on the bus and only three more *aliyos* to learn with Rashi. Whenever he went away from Yeshiva for *Shabbos*, he fell behind on the *parsha*. But that was part of having grandparents, his parents reminded him.

Sure, there was the Jewish Center downtown that his grandparents attended to socialize, but there was nothing like family, and every grandchild who was old enough took turns visiting for *Shab-*

bos. And visiting meant chatting through the meals, meeting their elderly friends, and being on the receiving end of lots and lots of good advice about who to marry and where to invest and how to treat family. It didn't leave a lot of time for learning. But, if he'd concentrate, he was sure he could have the *parsha* completed before he arrived back in New York. Then he could unpack and take a leisurely shower. That was something to look forward to on this muggy summer day.

"You don't have to worry about the fog," the man continued, breaking into Yitzy's thoughts. "I've been taking this route in to New York City once a week for the past half-a-year. Yep, every Sunday I'm on this bus route. And this driver -- his name is Bob – he's the best. He knows every turn, every curve, every bump on the road. This winter I was on the bus during that huge storm in January -- remember that storm?"

Yitzy nodded and glanced at the *chumash* page open in front of him. Only three more *aliyos*. Why did he have to get a seatmate who needed a friend?

"We left New Haven when the sky was threatening, but no one believed that the snow would come down so heavy and so fast. By the time we reached midway through Connecticut, the roads were covered. But Bob? He handled the bus like a pro. The ride was a little slow, but he made it to New York without even a delay. Yep. Bob's a winner." The man's voice was low and gravely, and he spoke slowly in a way that seemed that he was used to people listening to him.

"Uh, that's good," Yitzy answered. Then he was quiet. He wasn't in the habit of getting into conversations with strangers. His favorite people to talk to were normal people: fifteen year old *yeshiva bachurim*. He already used up all his good manners on *Shabbos* chatting with his grandparents about the weather, and the food they ate, and their sleeping schedules. Yitzy leaned closer to the window and tried to concentrate on his learning.

"Yep. That trip was memorable," the man continued rambling.

"'Course then I was happy 'cause my brother talked to me. I'm hoping for that today, too. Last two weeks, I couldn't get a word out of him. Still, you can't help but hope, isn't that so?" The man's gaze rested on Yitzy... waiting.

Yitzy looked at the man, wondering. Why wouldn't the man's own brother talk to him? He was a thin, clean cut man, looking about fifty-five years old and wearing a casual, blue, button-down shirt, blue jeans, and sneakers without socks. Yitzy could see the pack of cigarettes peeking out of the man's shirt pocket, and the daily newspaper folded on his lap. Sandy blond hair, topped by sunglasses, lay combed to cover a bald patch on his head. Altogether, his features were nothing unusual. What was different--very different, and a little disconcerting--was how his searching blue eyes focused intently on Yitzy.

"Yep. A person can't but hope," the man sighed. "Traveling alone?"

"Yeah," said Yitzy, feeling a little uncomfortable, and shifting in his seat.

"You're going in to New York, right?"

"Uh, yeah."

There was a pause. "You want to know how I know? I only got this bus in New Haven, right? So how did I know you're headed to New York? I could have guessed you're getting a connection to Atlantic City, right?" The man chuckled.

Yitzy shrugged. His eyes skimmed the rest of the bus. Why'd this guy sit next to him, of all people? There were plenty of other empty seats. Should he get up and move?

"I know it because I see plenty of junior rabbis when I go in to New York City. New York is full of them. But I don't see them on the bus too often. What're you doing up in New England?"

"I'm coming from my grandparents," Yitzy said. "They live in Hartford and they usually drive me back to *yeshiva*... uh, school, when I visit them, but today they couldn't drive because of the weather. Um... would you mind if I would go back to my reading now?"

Fog

That morning, he had assured his grandmother that taking a public bus was no problem. He was in 10th grade already, and he could easily navigate Port Authority Bus Terminal alone when the bus pulled in.

His grandfather agreed. "I went on the subway alone when I was six years old," he told Yitzy's Bubby.

"The world was different then," she had replied.

"What was the big deal?" Yitzy had told his grandmother. He'd be fine. Kids his age even traveled to *Eretz Yisroel* all by themselves, he assured her. From Port Authority, he could take a subway train and be back in yeshiva in time for *mincha*, with plenty of time to spare.

At last, after wrapping up some left over marble cake and a chunk of gefilte fish, with a fork and napkin, just in case, his grandmother finally agreed. "But call when you get there," she said.

Yitzy looked back into his *chumash* and tried to remember where he was up to.

"Sure. You can read," the man said. "All the junior rabbis -- they all read. I see 'em on the subways with open books all the time. Maybe with all your reading, you'll even find an answer for my question. It's a good question for a rabbi, you know. Even a rabbi in training." The man sat back and folded his arms.

Yitzy tried to concentrate. Minutes passed. Finally he turned to the man. "Okay, so what's your question? But," he hastened to add, "I'm not a rabbi. I'm not even a rabbi in training. I'm going to be an accountant."

The man smiled. "In my book, anyone who wears a suit jacket and a black hat in July is a rabbi. My question is about my brother who I'm going to visit in New York. My younger brother, Fred. He was always the good one. He was the one who did well in school, who graduated first in the class, and went on to college. Me, I stayed at home in New Haven and worked for my father selling furniture. I wanted to make money. But Fred, he was always helping people. Born that way, I guess. You know the type. I even remember him helping out old Mr. Fisher when he couldn't rake his leaves alone anymore or shovel his walk. Didn't do it for money, either.

"Anyways, it didn't surprise anyone that Fred went to school and became a social worker. First he worked around different agencies, trying to make life easier for old people, immigrants, people who were sick. Recently, though, he decided he really wanted to help kids, 'cause, like he'd say, that's like working with the roots to make a healthy tree. You get the picture."

Yitzy nodded, wondering where all this was going. He glanced out the window. His grandfather wouldn't have enjoyed driving through this grey cloud. He closed his *chumash* over his finger, still hoping to finish at least one more *aliya*.

"Anyways, Fred got himself a job just two years ago in New York City. He helped all kinds of kids with tough lives. Inner-city kids – that type. He understood them, and tried to turn them around. He really cared."

The man paused for a moment, and closed his eyes. Then he continued. "Me—I'm not so good. When we were kids, we used to sing a song about 'only the good die young.'" He hummed a bit. "You don't know that song, do you? But when I heard that song the first time, I went out and stole a pack of gum from Shoprite. I didn't want to be too good.

"But Fred, he was always good. So good that he never dreamed that the six-foot-two kid he was trying to help would beat him up in a school hallway. It was pretty bad. They brought him straight to Columbia Hospital a few blocks away from the school. And the kid went to juvenile court. 'I messed up,' the kid said. Just like that: 'messed up.'" The man frowned and clenched his fists.

Then he sighed and turned his hands hopelessly upward. "Fred's got a long stretch ahead. And so what can I do, besides go visit him once a week on my day off.

"So now," he said to Yitzy, "you look like you read lots of religious books. You tell me -- why?" The man's voice was strained, and his bright blue eyes looked pleadingly at Yitzy. "Tell me why

Fog

Freddie? What's my good little brother doing, lying in bed with a brain injury and fighting for his life?"

The man fell silent. He looked at Yitzy, waiting…

"Uh…"

Boy, did Yitzy feel dumb. Why couldn't the guy just ask him to explain a *tosfos* or something easy? He was only fifteen, after all. He never even visited a hospital… except when his mother had a baby, and even then he'd only looked through a glass window. What did he know about really sick people?

Yitzy had a vague feeling this had something to do with what they discussed in seventh grade when the class wanted to waste time and they'd get Rabbi Hoffberg off the topic by asking him questions about *tzaddik vera lo* and *rasha vetov lo*. He could still hear his friend Shimmy's voice raised: 'But what do you *mean*, Rabbi Hoffberg? Why does *Hashem* allow bad people to be rich and famous? And how come good people suffer?' He remembered that lessons like those twisted and meandered on and on – often pushing off a test until the next day. Sometimes Rabbi Hoffberg threw in something to do with suffering being an atonement, and rewards given in this world taking away from *olam haba*. Sometimes there were amazing stories where what appeared to be bad actually turned out to be the greatest blessing in the person's life, and sometimes there were allusions to *gilgulim* and other worlds. But in the end, the answer always boiled down to the fact that limited human beings are by definition incapable of understanding *Hashem's* ways. Shimmy always claimed that wasn't an answer, and Rabbi Hoffberg said that people who believe can live with questions.

"Uh… I think that, uh…"

What did this guy believe in? What did he want from Yitzy? How in the world could he start explain all of Rabbi Hoffberg's classes to a stranger? Too bad Shimmy wasn't here. He was the talk-y type.

"Uh… See, we're just little people," Yitzy said. "We don't know how G-d runs the world. We just have to do what we're supposed to and, uh... like you said, there's always hope."

"So you're saying you don't have an answer." The man sighed. "No one has an answer for me. My minister doesn't have any answers, either."

The man sighed again and closed his eyes. Yitzy looked back into his *chumash*. Still three more *aliyos* to go. He tried to learn, but his heart went out to the man. Sure, he was a stranger, but suffering was written all over his face, embedded in his eyes, and Yitzy kind of wished he could help. But what should he say? Maybe your brother shouldn't have been in that hallway alone? Or maybe your brother is suffering because you stole a pack of gum? Give it back and maybe he'll get well? He had no clue.

Yitzy looked out the window. The bus had entered the city and twisted along the bumpy streets. Traffic was getting heavier as the bus traveled through the Bronx and closer to New York City. The fog choked the brick apartment buildings built on the edge of the highway, with their broken windows and stacks of fire escapes assembled like tinker-toys. People hung out the windows, and he could see pillows arranged on the fire escapes for the inhabitants on the higher floors to get a little air. He wondered if the six-foot-two student grew up around here.

The man stretched and opened his eyes. "I can feel we're getting close. Even Bob can't keep the bumps out of the road."

"Yeah. Looks like we're almost there," Yitzy said. "Uh...if you'd like, uh...I'll add your brother to my prayers. I mean, if you want..."

The man thought. "You know what? That would be awesome. I'm not a big prayer person myself, but maybe G-d would listen to someone like you who prays all the time."

The audio system, which until then had been playing soft music, suddenly sputtered to life. "George Washington Bus Terminal," Bob announced over the loudspeaker. "GW Bridge Terminal. Next stop, Port Authority."

"Well, enjoy your reading," the man said. "And maybe we'll

meet again."

"Maybe next time you'll ask me an easier question." Yitzy half mumbled.

"Praying for my brother is the kindest thing you could offer. I'm gonna tell Freddie that today he's got a junior rabbi praying for him."

The man stood, held on to the seat and made his way down the aisle in the moving bus. It pulled into the station as the man reached the front. "Thanks, Bob," he said. Then he pushed his sunglasses over his eyes, climbed down the steps and exited onto the pavement. As the bus headed back onto the roads and down toward Port Authority, the man turned, and waved. Yitzy waved back through the window and then the man was swallowed by the city crowd.

After an hour, Yitzy arrived in yeshiva just in time for *mincha*. He felt kind of funny *davening* for a stranger – a stranger's brother, that was – but he made sure to add 'Fred' into a heartfelt *refa'enu*. Then he dropped off his stuff in the dorm and went to the public phone in the hall to call his grandparents.

"Hi, Zaidy. It's Yitzy. Safe and sound. Just finished *mincha*."

"So good to hear, Yitzy. How was the weather? How was the trip?"

"Well, it sure was incredibly foggy." Yitzy leaned against the wall. It had been quite a trip. "Interesting guy sitting next to me."

His grandfather chuckled. "That's part of public transportation. You meet all kinds of different types of people out there in the world, and they each have a story."

"You can say that again," Yitzy sighed.

"But you're old enough to handle it. You know who you are, and how to make a *kiddush Hashem* wherever you go."

Yitzy smiled a bit. "Yeah. I guess you're right, Zaidy. Thanks for having me again, and please thank Bubby again, especially for the marble cake."

"The pleasure was ours. Take care, Yitzy. Learn well."

"Yes," he told himself as he hung up. "I think I will."

The Other Side of the Desk

SURI SQUIRMED IN HER CHAIR, fiddled nervously with her spoon, and, oblivious to the soggy state of her breakfast cereal, tearfully poured out her heart to her mother. "But what if they don't put me in the same class as Miriam?" she whimpered. "And what if I'm in the room with the broken radiator and I'm cold all year? And what if... what if my teacher doesn't like me?" She frowned, put down her spoon, and a great big tear ran down her cheek, threatening to add salt to the sugary cereal at the end of its path.

Mommy passed a tissue to her little daughter. "We've been through this before," she said, "but I'll tell you all the answers again, okay? Just start eating because otherwise you'll be late for the first day of school."

As Suri nibbled listlessly, Mommy began. "Number one: there's only one class in your grade. I don't know where you got all this worrying about who's going to be in your class. As long as Miriam didn't change schools...."

Suri looked up suddenly, eyes wide.

Mommy laughed, "Which she didn't – I just spoke with her mother this morning about the bus route – so you both will be in the very same second grade classroom. Number two: the janitor in school spends the whole summer fixing things that were broken. The radiator should be working fine, and just in case it's not, you can wear a sweater. And number three: teachers like all the kids in their class."

Suri looked up, suspicious. "Are you sure?"

"Of course," Mommy said. "You have a smile that no one can resist! Your teacher will love you. You're the sweetest, smartest, cutest Suri in the whole entire world!"

Suri thought about it, chewed up the last spoon of cereal and then grinned. "Okay. I'm ready to go. I don't want to be late for the first day."

Devorah Leah swung her brand new leather teacher's briefcase over her shoulder and glanced in the mirror on the way out the door. This was her first day going to good old Bnos Chayil wearing the clothing of her choice – a soft pink sweater and a pleated grey skirt – instead of a checkered uniform skirt. Did she look as nervous as she felt? Is this how all new teachers start their very first day on the other side of the desk? Is this how *her* teachers used to feel? She never thought about them as people before. She put a serious look on her face and scrunched her eyebrows together. One thing she remembered from all the lessons in Bnos Tzlofchod Seminary was that teachers were never supposed to smile, especially on the first day of school. If you'd smile at the kids the first day, you'd be chopped meat.

She adjusted her headband, and patted down her collar. *Good morning, Miss Rosen,* she whispered with a serious look. She glanced at her watch. She still had a few extra minutes. Maybe she'd look more like a teacher in her lavender sweater? Then she laughed. I can't believe I'm doing this. I already picked out what to wear in the middle of the summer. She firmly grasped the leather strap of her briefcase, opened the front door and started her walk to school.

★★★

"Have a great day, Suri," Mommy said, when she saw the bus appear in the distance.

Suri turned back from her place in line. "Mommy... can't you come into the classroom with me? Last year you did."

"Last year you were in first grade and we had orientation. This year, you start with all the big girls. Look! There's Miriam, sitting in the front row of the bus. She's saving a seat for you. You'll be just fine. Go ahead. I'll be waiting right here at the bus stop when you come home."

Suri climbed onto the school bus, and watched her Mommy waving and waving until she disappeared in the distance.

★★★

Devorah Leah took a deep breath, and marched toward the teacher's room at the far end of the hall which had been off limits until today. Pushing open the door, she was surrounded by a cacophony of voices.

"Does anyone know how to work the copy machine?"

"I need a cup of coffee. It looks like I'm in the room with the broken radiator."

Devorah Leah smiled shyly at one of the women who she recognized as her old teacher from her student years at Bnos Chayil. She wondered if the older, experienced teachers got nervous on the first day of school. Maybe her former teacher could help her cross the great divide between the student population and the world of teachers. "Hi, Mrs. Griller," she said timidly.

"Why, hello! Devorah Leah Rosen! I heard that you were joining the staff this year. Good luck with the second grade. They're a very nice class. I taught them last year when they were in first grade."

Devorah Leah smiled. "Thank you. Any last minute tips?"

The first bell rang and the teachers gathered their supplies and scattered to their workplaces. "Remember not to smile," Mrs.

Griller said as they parted ways.

Devorah Leah walked down the hall to 'her' classroom and glanced proudly at the welcome poster she had hung on the doorway. Twenty three butterflies with girls' names on them flew in a circle on the pale blue poster board. I hope the girls are as obedient as the butterflies, Devorah Leah mused. She peeked into the room. When all twenty three girls were standing quietly by their desks, she strode to the teacher's desk and put down her briefcase. Good grief! What am I doing on this side of the desk? she thought.

"Ahem. Good morning, girls," she said. "My name is Miss Rosen. Please answer 'hinieni' when I call your name."

Don't smile, don't smile, don't smile, Devorah Leah reminded herself as she read each name.

Smile, smile, smile, thought little Suri in the front row. The teacher won't be able to resist my smile.

"Suri Flitchkin?"

"Hineini!" she said eagerly with a grin. But the teacher didn't smile back.

★★★

"Look! There's our teacher!" Suri said to Miriam, pressing her forehead to the window pane on the bus.

"Yeah. Looks like she's walking home."

"I like her sweater," Suri continued.

"Yeah. Pink is my favorite color."

"Yeah. Mine too."

"And we both got erasers today for writing our names. I think I like her," Miriam said.

"Yeah, I think I like her too," Suri said. "But she's a little scary." And I don't know if she likes me, she sighed.

★★★

"So how was your first day?" Mrs. Griller asked Devorah Leah in the teachers' room the next morning.

"I... I think it was okay. But I just don't feel like a real teacher. I think of myself as just a kid."

"A teacher has a special something," Mrs. Griller said thought-fully as they walked down the hall to their respective classrooms. "Your students will see it even if you don't know it yourself."

At the end of the day, Miss Rosen made an announcement. "Tomorrow we'll have our first quiz," she said firmly. "Please re-member to take home your *chumash* sheets so you can study."

Twenty-three little heads bobbed up and down. Their little hands fluttered into their folders, pulling out the two pages they needed, and sliding them into their homework notebooks. They're just like the butterflies on my poster, Devorah Leah thought. She worked hard, however, not to smile. She just nodded, and watched as the girls flitted by the poster, one by one.

Then, when the class was empty, she threw away a few stray scraps left over from the day's project, picked up her briefcase, and turned off the lights. I know I'm not supposed to care, but I can't help wondering if they like me, she thought.

It was funny what that wide, wooden desk could do. Solidly standing between one woman and twenty-plus kids, it divided them into two different species. On one side was a teacher who the children expected to guide them and know all the answers. On the other side was a mush of personalities, backgrounds, hair colors, abilities and disabilities that the teacher saw as "the class." The class needed a good teacher so they could learn. The teacher needed discipline so she could teach.

And yet...

On each side of the desk, there were really just people. Per-haps some were teacher-people, with more knowledge, experi-ence, and qualifications who came to school to lead. And perhaps some were student-people, with ideas and *middos* yet unformed, who came to school to learn from more about the world and to grow from the experience. But on both sides of the desk were people. People with hearts. Hearts that held real human feelings. Feelings that stayed hidden. Most of the time....

"There she goes," Suri said, looking out the window.

"Yeah. And our quizzes are inside her briefcase. I hope I got the right answers. I studied so-o-o hard."

"Yeah. Me too." And I hope she reads the note I wrote her on the back of the paper, Suri worried. And I hope she likes it....

★★★

Correcting tests is an entirely differnt part of the job, Devorah Leah thought to herself, scrawling large checks down the side of the page. "*Vayomer, hu amar, Vayomru, hem omru....*" This is pretty boring. It has nothing to do with teaching. Maybe I could even pay a friend to do this for me next time.... She hummed a bit to herself as she checked paper after paper, trying to finish the task. And, as she jotted down the scores in her mark book, she was surprised that she actually could match up the faces to the names after just four days of school.

She was pleased to see 100% for Suri – the cute girl in the front row. Just thinking about Suri made Devorah Leah happy that she chose to teach this year. She enjoyed watching Suri's little face reflect all the emotion that she put into the lesson. When she taught about *Rosh Hashana*, Suri looked so enthralled. Devorah Leah noticed how she sat up straight in her chair when she mentioned how *Hashem* was the king of the whole world and could see them all the time.

She turned the paper face down on the pile and was about to go on to the next page when she saw that Suri had written something on the back. Was it more vocabulary sentences?

She held the paper close to read the small, light pencil marks. "Dear Miss Rosen, do you like me? I don't know if you like me. I like you. I love you. Love, Suri."

That was a surprise! It was a good thing she was putting the effort into correcting the tests herself! But why would Suri even think that she didn't like her? She actually noticed that today, little Suri wasn't smiling. That big, irresistible grin had been absent all day from her little face. As a matter of fact, she had hardly spoken at all.

It must be because of my no-smiling policy! I probably scared the poor kid! Devorah Leah realized. But what can I do? She chewed her pen for a moment and then wrote back. "Dear Suri, Of course I like you. And I missed your smile today. Your loving teacher, Miss Rosen."

★★★

"Good morning, class," said Miss Rosen. In what was becoming routine, she walked into the classroom and stepped to her side of the teacher's desk. Then she read the role, nodding at each "*heneini.*"

"I enjoyed correcting your tests last night," she continued. "I'm going to pass them back now. You all did very nicely. Remember to take your test home to show your mother, and then bring it back so we can keep it in your test folder. Okay, Faidle, Ruchy, Yehudis, Suri…" As she handed back the test, she thought, I hope she reads the note that I wrote on the back of the paper, and I hope she likes it….

Out of the corner of her eye she saw Suri flip over her test, and watched her read, slowly mouthing the words she wrote the night before. Then Suri looked up… until her eyes met Miss Rosen's. Miss Rosen gave her a tiny, tiny smile. Suri blushed – and then she smiled broadly.

Devorah Leah's eyebrows shot up. "Suri! You lost a tooth!"

"The dentitht took it out. It wathent falling out and it wath hurting. Thath why I couldn't thmile yethterday."

So that's why she wasn't smiling, Devorah Leah practically laughed. Her heart felt much lighter. She was happy that Suri's smile was back, even with the slight hole at the center.

★★★

"Miriam! Look!" Suri said, pointing across the playground on *Shabbos* afternoon. "It's Miss Rosen! She sitting on the bench over there."

Miriam climbed up to the top of the jungle gym and stared and stared… and then started giggling.

"What's so funny?" Suri asked from the ground.

"Teachers are supposed to be teachers, not regular people. Only regular people go to the park."

"So? Teachers are people, too. I once saw Mrs. Griller in a snood instead of a *sheitle!*"

Miriam laughed out loud, and suddenly Miss Rosen looked up. Miriam scampered down as fast as she could. "Oh, no! She saw us!"

"Come on," Suri said. "Let's go say 'Good *Shabbos.*'"

"I'm so embarrassed!" Miriam said but Suri took her hand and practically dragged her to the slide.

"Good *Shabbos*, Miss Rosen," Suri said.

"Good *Shabbos,*" Miriam managed to squeak.

"Good *Shabbos*, girls," Devorah Leah said.

The girls nodded and blushed and, having run out of conversation, ran back to the jungle gym. "You see," Suri panted. "She's a regular person. I told you so."

"I liked her *Shabbos* shoes."

"Yeah. And did you see the buttons on her shirt?"

"Yup. I can't wait to tell the whole class that we saw Miss Rosen on *Shabbos!*" They both climbed to the top of the jungle gym and tried very hard to pretend they were looking the other way, but continued to glance over and over again in the direction from which they had just fled.

That was funny, Devorah Leah thought, watching them watch her every move. I remember feeling the same way about my teachers so I guess that means I'm a real teacher, too. And, hiding a very small smile, she stood, and headed home.

U R Unique

SHLOIMY QUICKLY HELPED CLEAR the last of the *cholent* plates from the table, and put the dirty silverware into the sink. In the Kreamstein family, it was the boys' job to clear the *Shabbos* table, since it was the girl's job to set the table while the boys were in *shul*. Shloimy stood by the door and took one more glance at his little brother sitting on the floor. "Come on, Chaim," he urged. "Bring in the last plate of pickles and Mommy will serve dessert. You want dessert, right?"

Chaim looked up from his game. He had just finished arranging all the little *menchies* in his Lego set in rows. "Huh?"

"Chaim, get up and help!" insisted Shloimy as he returned to the table, having cleared all the other dishes by himself.

"Oh, Shloimy," said Faige from seat, "I'll do it already. You know it's hard to get Chaim to do anything." She reached for the last offending plate and swooped it off the table.

"But you're spoiling him," insisted Shloimy as he followed Faige to kitchen. "When I was ten, I helped tons more than he does."

Faige just shrugged. "It's easier to move the plate than to get him to move."

"I could have done it too, Faige," Shloimy argued, "but it's not right for *him*!"

Mommy came into the kitchen just at the moment, before the old argument could play itself to its end. "Thanks for your help… both of you. Go ahead back to the table now and help Tatty sing *"Tzur Meshelo."* Dessert will be served shortly. And Shloimy--Tatty and I would like to speak to you privately after the *seuda*, before you go to learn."

As Shloimy joined in the *zemiros* with the rest of the family, he wondered what the secret discussion would be about. Yeshiva? He mentally reviewed how he was doing in each subject. Had any Rebbe called with a complaint or compliment this week? He couldn't think of anything specific. He worked hard in all his subjects and he was near the top of the class, well-liked by his classmates, cheerful enough, generally cooperative. If anything, he was too bright, he mused. Maybe it was about summer plans. Camp? A trip to *Eretz Yisroel*? Shloimy was curious: what could the private topic be?

Mommy served each child a slice of apple cake with a scoop of ice cream. Faige, who was on a diet with the rest of her junior high school class, slid her ice cream onto Shulamis' plate. Shulamis happily gobbled up the entire plate and asked for more, just like the rest of her fourth grade classmates would have done. Chani quietly licked the ice cream off her spoon as she turned page after page of the latest *frum* novel under the table. Pinny banged his spoon on the high chair with one hand and put the ice cream into his mouth with the other. Shloimy finished his dessert and scraped the last of the sugary apple goop off his plate as he discussed a complicated Rashi on the *parsha* with Tatty. And Chaim?

"Chaim, come have your dessert," said Mommy.

"Huh?" Chaim had finished lining up all the blue and red Legos on the floor around the *menchies*. Now, it seemed, the *menchies* were at war, because Chaim took turns throwing a blue *menchie* at a red one and then vice-versa.

"Dessert, Chaim," said Tatty slowly.

"Oh, dessert! Yum!" Chaim quickly slid into his place, enjoyed dessert immensely, *bentched* with the family, and slid right back to his toys.

"Chaim's turn to clear the dessert plates," said Shloimy determinedly. "I did the rest of the entire meal."

Tatty got up and walked over to the major set-up on the floor. He squatted down next to Chaim. "Nice building," he commented.

Chaim looked up. "See, this is the red team and this is the blue team and they're fighting, but here's the Hatzolo station."

"It's great, Chaim. Now you have to take a break and clear the dishes…"

"Aww…."

"But then you can play until *Mincha*. Okay. Ready? Set? Now."

Chaim got up, glanced backwards at his toys, and began stacking the dirty cake plates.

"Shloimy," said Tatty, turning away from his youngest son, and facing his oldest, "Mommy and I would like to speak with you if you have a minute…"

"Uh, sure Tatty," said Shloimy. *What could this be about?* He wondered. *So serious!*

A few moments later, Shloimy sat alone with his mother and father in the study, with the door closed. The clock ticked in the background. The Shabbos noises of Shulamis and Chani playing Chinese jump rope with their neighbors, and of Faige chatting with her friends faded in the background. Shloimy looked at his parents. His father seemed to be composing his thoughts, his mother looked toward his father, waiting for him to start whatever conversation was about it begin.

As if reading his mind, Tatty began. "Shloimy, as our oldest son, we rely on you a lot. You're almost a third parent in the house, you know."

Shloimy knew it. He was the one who his parents trusted to finish jobs and help get things done. He had that sense of responsibility engraved in him since toddlerhood, always cleaning up his toys, never loosing his papers from school, always giving over phone messages accurately, and watching the little kids whenever his parents needed him. It was nice to have Faige in second place, he had to admit. She more than did her share. Still, he was the *bechor*, and being first-born did make him who he was today.

"Because of your position in the family," continued Tatty seriously, "we'd like to take you into confidence, so you can understand more of what's going on at home."

Mommy continued. "It's about Chaim."

Shloimy looked up, startled. Not about *him*? Not about Yeshiva, or camp or anything in *his* world?

"You may have noticed that Chaim's a little less than cooperative sometimes," Mommy said, her eyes filled with concern.

Shloimy grimaced. "You can say that again. That kid is as stubborn as a mule. He doesn't lift a finger to help. He just does his own thing all day long."

"Well, we've had him tested," Mommy said, taking a deep breath. "He's got a problem. It's not his fault."

"Go ahead," said Shloimy. "It's ADD, right?"

Tatty and Mommy both stared at Shloimy. Mommy opened her mouth, and closed it, opened it and closed it. Finally Tatty spoke for both of them. "How did *you* know?"

"Oh, it's obvious," said Shloimy. "Nowadays every other kid has ADD. We have at least two in my class."

"You're kidding," said Mommy.

"Well, well," said Tatty, taking a deep breath.

"You mean we shouldn't worry?" asked Mommy slowly.

Shloimy felt kind of funny, being asked for his opinion. "I mean, I'm not an expert or anything," he said, fidgeting, "it's just that there's help out there, and, well, I guess I'm happy you finally have a name for his problem." Shloimy glanced at the clock on the shelf. "Was there anything else you wanted to talk about? My *chavrusa* is going to be waiting…"

"That's it, Shloimy," said Tatty. "To us, this was pretty big news. We now have a handle on why Chaim is so different than the rest of you kids, and we're going to get help in educating him to be the best he can be."

Shloimy waited expectantly. *That was it? The big secret?*

Mommy turned to Tatty. "I guess kids these days handle things pretty well. To think we worried about telling him."

Shloimy gave his parents a big smile. "See you for *shalosh seudos*," he said, and he was off down the block toward *shul*.

Shloimy walked down the block, looking down at the sidewalk, thinking deeply. They were worried to tell me? So Chaim was officially labeled ADD: Attention Deficit Disorder. That meant that his brain worked differently than most other people. He would have a hard time paying attention to what the teacher said. He would probably rather be doing his own thing than following directions. School would be tough. But, Shloimy thought, the two most popular kids in my class are classified the same way. Everyone remembers the day in fifth grade when Shimmy announced to the class that he had three initials tacked to the end of his name that made him special, and then Tzvi one-upped him and said that he was ADHD, and that made him even more special. Shloimy smiled to himself, and looked up. He was at *shul* already.

"Good Shabbos, Shloimy," called Avi. "You're a few minutes late. I was wondering if I was going to have to come and drag you out of bed!"

"Nah, I wasn't sleeping," replied Shloimy. As the two boys found *gemara*s on the shelf and settled down to learn, Shloimy explained the delay. "My parents made this whole big deal that they wanted to talk to me after the *seuda*. It turns out that my brother Chaim was labeled ADD this week by some professional."

"So?"

"Yeah, that's what I said. My parents seemed kind of worried, but I'm sure he'll be okay. But you see, Avi, the thing that gets me, is that once you have a few letters strung after your name, you become something different."

"Well, wasn't he different already? Every Shabbos afternoon we learn together, you complain about how you just finished clearing the whole table, and how Chaim never helps."

"Yeah, he's different in his own way and I'm happy he'll get some special help, and that my parents will get to understand him better. But it's those *letters* that get me."

"You mean, he's not regular Chaim-who-needs-to-learn-to-cooperate. He's a different category of human being. Like my Aunt Judy. She got a college degree recently. Now she's an B.A. All of a sudden she's a different person. You think I see a difference? She seems like the same Aunt Judy to me, only now she can make more money at a job. But all the grown-ups around her all of a sudden think she's something special."

"Exactly," agreed Shloimy.

Avi thought. "You know, I've seen some people with really long lists of letters after their name, like doctors with their PhD., M.D., LCSW... all sorts of stuff. No one even knows what the letters stand for."

Shloimy smiled. "So you know what I'm thinking...?"

Avi grinned, "After being your *chavrusa* for five years, I think that I know what you're thinking... and you're nuts."

Shloimy laughed. "Come on. Let's learn already." He opened the *gemara* and began reading to read aloud.

***

The plan was already hatching in Shloimy's mind. If Chaim's attention span was short, Shloimy suffered from a different kind of Attention Deficit Disorder too. He was deficient in *receiving* attention. He never *got* enough attention for the things he did right. As he walked home from *shul*, he mulled over the situation. What would it take for *him* to be special and different, to see that look of care and concern in his parents' eyes when they mentioned *his* name, to have a team of people design a learning program for *him*, to have initials at the end of *his* name...

That was it! He needed some letters attached at the end of Shloimy Kreamstein that would make people take note, and think to themselves: "Ah! Here's a boy that deserves our attention. He's one of a kind, that Shloimy!"

But what did he want to stand out about? What *did* make him different? Shloimy thought long and hard all through *shalosh seudos*, and right through *havdala*. Then he went to his room, and grabbed a lined sheet of paper and numbered the lines one through five. Between chewing on his pencil and staring at the wall, Shloimy wrote:

1.   Shloimy Kreamstein, T.N. (Top Notch)
2.   Shloimy Kreamstein, V.C. (Very Cool)
3.   Shloimy Kreamstein, B.B. (Best *bachur*)
4.   Shloimy Kreamstein, L.O.T.C. (Leader of the Class)
5.   Shloimy Kreimstein, I.G. (Incredible Genius)

He turned the paper upside down on his desk and went downstairs to see what was for *melave malka*.

"Oh, Shloimy," said Mommy, as she stood by the sink washing dishes. "I was wondering where you were. Could you please take out the garbage?"

"Sure, Mommy," he said. As he lifted the bag from the garbage can, he noted that something was leaking out. "Hey, Chani," he called to his sister who was already in the middle of a steaming bowl of oatmeal (and another novel), "bring me another garbage bag quick so I don't drip this stuff all over the floor."

Chani pulled herself out of her book and ran to help as Mommy looked on gratefully. "That was a brilliant idea, Shloimy," Mommy commented. "Not everyone would have cared to do that right."

Shloimy smiled. "My pleasure. What's there to eat?"

"Pizza in the freezer, left over challa to wash if you'd like. Or oatmeal. The usual," answered Faige.

"Well let's make something a bit unusual," said Shloimy. "How about raisins in the oatmeal? Or olives on the pizza?"

"What about broccoli on the pizza too?" asked Faige.

Suddenly a dull Melave Malka became a festive meal. Shloimy took out six slices of pizza and topped them with olives, broccoli, slices of onion, hot peppers, and extra cheese, and popped them into the oven.

When everything was finished to the last crumb, Tatty turned to Shloimy and commented, "This was the best Melave Malka I've had in decades. Where'd you find this recipe?"

"Oh, it's original," replied Shloimy.

"Well, you're one talented kid," said Tatty appreciatively. "I predict a dazzling future."

Shloimy grinned. He couldn't help but agree.

When Shloimy went upstairs to get ready for bed, he saw his overturned list waiting patiently on the desk. It was decision-making time. Time to give himself a title. Hhhhmmm. Top Notch? Too general. Very Cool? Eh... He wasn't *so* cool, really. Maybe lukewarm. Best *Bachur*? Not compared to Avi. Leader of the Class? It just wasn't true. But Incredible Genius? He *was* very smart. Everyone said so. Genius might be stretching it, but he could grow into the name. Incredible Genius it would be.

The next day in Yeshiva, when Shloimy signed his name at the top of his *parsha* test, he wrote Shloimy Kreamstein, I.G. Later that day, when the boys passed around a card for everyone to sign for a sick classmate, he used his newfound title again. And, when the math teacher wasn't looking, he filled in I.G. after his name on the teacher's seating chart.

But having a title wasn't enough, Shloimy began to realize. It wouldn't be enough just to have the initials. It helped, of course, to make him stand out, and set him above the pack. But he'd have to act the part as well. It wouldn't be hard, he thought, to add a few *illuyish* practices into his daily life, the type of actions that only genius' could get away with. He'd just have to do a few things that his future biographers would be able to add to their best selling books about how a genius was raised.

On the way home from Yeshiva that day, Shloimy took along his *gemara* to learn on the street. After all, it did say that one should learn "while walking on the road." He looked into the *gemara* and started reviewing the morning's learning. Then, he took a quick peek around him. Yes, there were enough boys standing nearby to notice him. He put his head back down into the *gemara* and furrowed his brow. Then, he took another furtive look upward. Good. There was a tree ahead of him, a little to the right of the sidewalk. He took a few more steps and ...

Ooof!

"Are you okay, Shloimy?" Nochum and Dovid came running.

"Uh, sure," said Shloimy, a bit dazed.

"Why'd you walk into the tree?" asked Dovid. "What did it ever do to you?"

"Well… I was just wondering why Abaye didn't answer Rava with the obvious answer that the ox must have been wounded when it ran…" Shloimy looked up at his friends.

"You're still thinking about that *gemara* we learned this morning?" said Nochum, a tinge of admiration in his voice..

"Oh, it's nothing. Just on my mind, that's all," said Shloimy as he stood up and brushed himself off. As he walked away with the *gemara* now folded closed under his arm, he could feel a lump forming on his forehead. But it was worth it. He had to earn his title.

The next day, Shloimy came to yeshiva without socks. Imagine: he was so distracted by his learning that he forgot socks. A perfect indication of what the I.G. stood for after his name. During *davening*, Avi noticed. "Mmmhm.. uh… *nu?*" he said to Shloimy, pointing to his bare ankles. Shloimy heard him, but continued swaying with even more devotion, *davening* with lots of energy. After the boys put away their *tefillin*, and the whole class was on their way down to breakfast, Avi asked him point blank. "Where're your socks, Shloimy?"

Nochum pulled a bit at the hem of Shloimy's pants to verify

the validity of Avi's question. Unfortunately, this was not a good trick to perform on a downward staircase. Shloimy tumbled and the whole class stumbled like dominos until, at the bottom of the stairs, Yisroel fell right into the cook who was carrying a full pot of farina to the table.

"What's going on here?!" the cook shouted, as the farina slid and slopped and finally spread itself across the lunch room floor.

It took only a few minutes to unravel the story, and push Shloimy up to the front of the line where the cook confronted him. "Where *are* your socks?" the cook shouted when he heard the story.

Shloimy looked down as if he had never heard of socks, as if his ankles weren't freezing cold since the moment he set foot outside his house. "Oh! My socks! I…I must have forgotten them. You see, if Rabbi Akiva and Rabbi Tarfon were both arguing with Rabbi Yochonon, it would appear that they were both taking the lenient view. However, on the next page of the *gemara*, we find that Rabbi Yonchonon lent his cow to Rabbi Akiva, which would seem to indicate that…"

The cook waved his hand. He was used to Yeshiva boys. "Get outta here, and put on a pair of socks," he yelled as he walked away to find a mop. But Nochum's eyes grew wide, and he whispered to the boys around him. "You know, I think Shloimy is really an *illuy*. You see how he's so wrapped up in his learning?"

"Hey, Shloimy," called Yankle, as Shloimy sat down to eat breakfast, with a *gemara* open in front of him, "you think I could be your *chavrusa* next time we switch?"

"Yeah, sure. Just remind me…" Shloimy looked up, tilted his head and squinted a bit. "You know, I sometimes loose track of such stuff."

Yankle walked away, and Shloimy could hear him bragging to Nochum who his next *chavrusa* would be. Shloimy took a pen from his shirt pocket to start jotting notes in the side of his *gemara* page. Then he flipped to the front cover, just to check. Yes, this was his *gemara*, with his name written in it. He stopped just for a moment to add I.G. with a flourish after his name, and then went back to his studies

The very next morning, Shloimy, open *gemara* in his hand, left his house with socks, but with his hat backwards, every other button undone and carrying an empty shopping bag for the lunch he left at home.

Avi pounced on him from behind the mailbox. "Alright, Shloimy. Why do you look like you're dressed for Purim? What's with the personality change?"

Shloimy looked at Avi with an uncomprehending look. "Are you talking about the change between Rav Huna's opinion in the opening phrases in the *gemara* and what he's holding by on the following page?"

Avi grabbed the *gemara* and opened it to the front cover. "What's this Shloimy Kreamstein, I.G. business? Come on, the truth." Avi planted himself firmly in front of Shloimy, *gemara* in his folded arms. "The whole truth and nothing but the truth."

"Aw, come on Avi," said Shloimy, reaching for his *gemara*. He could feel his career as a genius rapidly coming to a close. Good old Avi was about to bring him back down to earth.

"Look," said Avi. "I know what you're up to, and more than one person can play this game. Wait until the class hears about this. It's going to be Nochum Beiner, S.T.C. (Sweet as They Come), and Yankle Torner, T.O.R.L. (Torah Only for the Rest of his Life), and me, Avi Zillinger, B.W. (Braces Wearer), and Yisroel Kramer, F.S."

"What's the F.S.?" asked Shoimy weakly.

"Farina Spiller. Come on, Shloimy. Give it up. Be normal."

Shloimy sighed, turned his hat around and buttoned his shirt. Avi handed him back his *gemara* and the two boys walked to Yeshiva together.

"It still gets me, though," said Shloimy. "The idea that putting letters after your name makes you so special and different. My brother is special and I'm just a Plain Nobody. Shloimy Kream-stein, P.N."

"Well, I have a proposal," said Avi. "Look at it this way. I think that everyone should add 'U.I.' after their name."

"What's that stand for?"

"Unique Individual," answered Avi.

Shloimy thought about it. If everyone was a U.I., then so were ADDs and ADHDs and MD's and PhDs -- and so was he! Each and every person was someone unique, even if their differences couldn't be labeled and fit into neat categories. He was unique too, in a really kind of nice way, and so was Avi.

Avi was right on target. "You're really something special, Avi," he said sincerely to his friend.

"Nah," Avi laughed. "I'm just a regular, normal guy. That's good enough for me!"

And, together with all the other regular, normal U.I.'s, the boys went off to school.